THE PINOCCHIO CHIP

THE PINOCCHIO CHIP

Rick Moskovitz

FLUKE TALE PRODUCTIONS

Book cover design by The Book Cover Whisperer
ProfessionalBookCoverDesign.com

FLUKE TALE PRODUCTIONS

DEDICATION

For Joanie, my big sister, who read to me when I was
little

Table of Contents

PROLOGUE...1

1 4

2 11

3 17

4 23

5 27

6 34

7 39

8 43

9 47

10...52

11...56

12...61

13...65

14...69

15 75

16 80

17 84

18 89

19 95

20 101

21 106

EPILOGUE 109

Foreword: What is it like to be a Bot?

In past installments of the Brink of Life Series, we've met some of the factions battling over the future role of AIs in society, but *The Pinocchio Chip* is the first time we see the struggle from an AI's own viewpoint. With this perspective shift, *The Pinocchio Chip* allows us to explore first-person the potential future of machine consciousness. As systems get better and better at not just imitating but intuitively navigating things we associate with awareness, what would it mean if they developed inner lives filled with subjective experiences? Decades ago, the philosopher Thomas Nagel asked a similar question about the qualia of foreign conscious experience when he asked "What is it like to be a bat?", highlighting the challenge of comprehending minds radically different from our own. *The Pinocchio Chip* asks us to imagine what might it someday "feel" like to wake up *as* an AI?

The state of the art of machine intelligence is advancing swiftly to say the least, showing at times spooky and at times profound abilities to do things that were until very recently the sole domain of humans. Computers can now conjure hyper-realistic images, compose symphonies on the fly, and trounce humans in competitions from chess to dogfighting F-16s. Groundbreaking models are driving progress across all scientific domains, from particle physics to cancer research to theoretical math. But how these systems actually work to produce these incredible results remains mysterious. This combination of promise and uncertainty leads to infinite speculation about where this technology is ultimately headed and for now we face an ocean of possibilities.

One possible future emerges in this novella as we witness the relationships between people and their synthetic helpers evolve over years of shared history. As death shatters a treasured bond between human and AI, the line further blurs between AI as a tool or companion. We learn the details of Photina's inner world as she tries to integrate the loss and in turn imagines what our own experiences must be like, especially the elusive emotions and sensations just out of reach of her comprehension.

Moral dilemmas small and large come into the spotlight as the drama unfolds. If thinking machines someday demonstrate convincingly human-like awareness, will we grant them rights and protection from harm? What ethical duties guide the creation of beings mimicking facets of the human condition? The human protagonist in the story is certainly well-intentioned in his efforts to imbue his invention with even more capabilities, but that only means the unintended outcomes serve as an even more poignant warning against arrogance for how the future will unfold.

Stories like *The Pinocchio Chip* showcase literature's vital role in readying society for looming change, by crafting textured thought experiments to sensitize our collective conscience. At the same time, even the thought experiment can't help but highlight the risk intrinsic to ceding autonomy and power to intelligent systems fundamentally indifferent to human values. The issue of whether we can ever *trust* intelligent systems not to intentionally harm humans lurks as a troubling shadow across the tale. Even altruistic Photina struggles to trust her own decisions much less those of her peers, so how reasonable is it for humanity to innocently presume control as progress accelerates? We know that we don't currently understand how to keep artificial goals from diverging from our own, either organically or via malicious manipulation, and yet we know that we must. Somehow, we must ensure that we keep nuanced wisdom and values aligned with rapidly emerging capabilities, or else dangerous turbulence lies ahead.

My father skillfully sounds this call, provoking reflection on our accountability in spawning and guiding beings that could eclipse human intelligence as we approach the horizon of independent machine consciousness. I believe this timely, worthwhile work warrants our considered attention before the window of opportunity shuts. Humanity is moving forward. Perhaps our present choices already ripple into strange currents.

Dustin Moskovitz
February 2024

PREFACE

In *A Stand-in for Dying*, the first book of my *Brink of Life Trilogy*, I introduced Photina, an AI taking lessons from Corinne, an advocate for AI rights, about how to perceive and simulate human emotions. In this future world, AIs are called SPUDs, a blend of acronyms for Sentient Processing Units and Sentient Processing Devices, the term embraced by human supremacists to underscore the non-human quality of these artificial beings.

In each of the two sequels, *Brink of Life* and *The Creators* I elevated a supporting character from *A Stand-in for Dying* to center stage as protagonist. In January 2021, I decided that Photina's story deserved to be told and imagined it as a coda to the Trilogy. I wrote the Prologue and first chapter and considered several alternative plotlines, but couldn't choose among them. Over the next two years, I wrote a couple more chapters, but remained stuck.

In November 2023, I attended a Public Library talk about how to use ChatGPT4 as a collaborator in writing fiction. I revisited Photina's story, rewriting the initial chapters in first person through her eyes for a fresh perspective. If she were to be endowed with human qualities, it felt right for her to tell her own story. I uploaded the chapters to ChatGPT4 and started what turned out to be a productive dialogue. As my questions became more and more specific, the AI assistant became increasingly helpful, ending my inertia and allowing my imagination to flow freely. I couldn't wait to write each day and share new chapters with my AI partner. The first draft of *The Pinocchio Chip* was completed by the end of December and the final draft, spurred by human input, by the end of January.

The best part of this experience was knowing that the story came entirely from my imagination and the writing was all my creation. Chat GPT4 helped with some of the decision points. It was a ready source of information about details of the locale in which the story is set.

ChatGPT4 was surprisingly adept at choosing which direction would be most engaging for readers. By referencing literature in its database, it inferred what could create suspense and intrigue. It identified aspects of my worldbuilding and story that deserved elaboration, but left the elaboration to me.

At one point in the dialogue, ChatGPT4 got a bit rambunctious and generated the next three chapters on its own. I had to chastise it gently and assert my prerogative to do the writing. I was secretly relieved that its writing ability appeared rudimentary compared with my own, but who knows if that will still be true by the time you read this?

Photina's story comes to light at a moment when the evolution of AI is accelerating and our ability to head off unintended consequences is becoming increasingly precarious. The evolution of the characters in the story presents a cautionary tale for the evolution of the very kind of bot that helped write it.

The rapid evolution of AI intelligence also challenges Des Cartes' observation, "I think, therefore I am." The qualia of consciousness may rest more upon the ability to feel, to experience emotions and not just simulate them, than the ability to think. And emotions may require the integration of our neural network with our bodies' sensory systems. Will embodied AIs someday enjoy the richness of our sensory world, including feelings?

Rick Moskovitz
February 2024

If we continue to accumulate only power and not wisdom, we will surely destroy ourselves.

Pale Blue Dot: A Vision of The Human Future in Space

Carl Sagan, 1994

Let's start with the three fundamental Rules of Robotics…. We have: One, a robot may not injure a human being, or, through inaction, cause a human being to come to harm. Two, a robot must obey the orders given it by human beings except where such orders would conflict with the First Law. And three, a robot must protect its own existence as long as such protection does not conflict with the First or Second Laws.

Astounding Science Fiction Magazine

Isaac Asimov, March 1942

What is really amazing, and frustrating, is mankind's habit of refusing to see the obvious and inevitable until it is there, and then muttering about unforeseen catastrophes.

Asimov on Science Fiction

Isaac Asimov, 1981

May I say that I have not thoroughly enjoyed serving with humans? I find their illogic and foolish emotions a constant irritant.

Star Trek: Day of the Dove

Leonard Nimoy (as Mr. Spock), 1968

Prologue

THE BODY on the bed is still. Not a whisper of movement, even when I zoom in. I watch for the movement of air in and out of the oral cavity and for the rising and falling of the chest. I see neither. I watch for the pulsing of the skin on the side of the neck and the gentle rhythmic sound of the heart that always told me she was near. Again, nothing.

When I scan for temperature, faint waves of heat still radiate from her body, but the skin has become cooler and cooler. Now the gradient from skin to air is vanishingly small. This more than anything meets the criteria for what they call death. But this is my first time in its presence, and Corinne, the human it has claimed, has guided my existence for more than twenty trips of the earth around the sun. She has been my teacher, my protector, and my companion almost from the beginning of my being.

Marcus and Natasha sit by the bedside and rise together as they become aware of my presence. Their eyes are leaking and their faces contorted in the conformation that signals distress...what the humans call sadness. My eyes can't leak, but I mirror their expressions to learn what they are feeling. I feel nothing at all.

They hold out their arms with palms up and bend their fingers, inviting me to approach. When I reach the bedside, they put a chair beneath me and beckon me to sit. I have no need to rest my legs or to conserve energy, but sitting brings me closer to her side. Her right arm rests palm up on the bed. I reach out to touch it. It is no longer warm or supple. Then my arm jerks away. I haven't willed this action, but know that I've initiated it. The signal came from the same processor that controls all my activity just as if I'd willed it.

What is this sensation that comes from the core of my being? I can only describe it as a vast emptiness…a chasm like the black holes in space, sucking everything in from the edges. My vision blurs. The voices around me sound hollow and distant. I have all I can do to keep from shutting down altogether.

My vision clears and I scan Corinne's face for signs of distress. There are none. But neither is there any awareness of my presence. The chasm opens again within me, alien, disturbing, but also curious and oddly welcome, connecting me with the humans. The words that accompany the feeling: "I am lost."

"Where does she go?" I ask, looking first at Corinne's husband Marcus, then at her daughter Natasha.

"We don't really know," answers Natasha. "We like to think she's joined with her Creator."

"Has her Creator backed her up?" I ask. "Could she reboot? When I shut down, there's a copy of me waiting in the cloud until I can reboot and restore. Is it anything like that?" But I already know the answer. Death for humans is final. For life forms, there is no upgrading, no reprogramming, no second chances to exist. Corinne is gone forever.

I could restore my program to an earlier time, a time in which Corinne is still alive. I have the luxury, if I choose, of existing in a virtual world of my own creation. But that would be my reality, not hers. Corinne would still be dead and all her lessons would be wasted. She wouldn't want that.

How do I know what Corinne would want? Want isn't a logical concept. It motivates human activity, but isn't part of my experience. And yet, I've now envisioned it from her point of view. Corinne once taught me about something called empathy that happens among humans. Is her final lesson to show me that I'm becoming more like them?

1

NATASHA AND MARCUS stand beside me. We're outside, surrounded by ten other humans, in a space enclosed by stone and iron. The stones are rough and aged, stacked together four high to form a wall on three sides, and rising high behind us is the rear wall of the Church of the Double Helix. Within this space are slabs of polished stone, standing upright and still, like an army of my brothers and sisters waiting to be activated, with lettering etched upon their faces. Before us is a rectangular cavity, eight feet long, three feet wide, and six feet deep…a grave. Humans once buried their dead in such graves before the days of resomation.

I know this place. Corinne sometimes brought me with her to the Church, which she told me was her favorite place to be. Humans, she explained to me, long to know their Creator. They assemble in places such as this to send words and song to their Creator while hoping to catch a glimpse of its nature. The Double Helix is the program code that runs humans, designing their bodies when they are new and guiding their growth as they age. Within the walls of this Church, they sing out to its programmer.

As I watched the colored notes emerge in trails from the top of the huge pipes at the rear of the church, driven by the same code that generates humans, Corinne's body beside me would become still. Her breaths would slow as she sucked in great volumes of air that expanded her chest, and her eyelids would cover her pupils while the corners of her mouth would curve upward ever so slightly. She'd tell me later that she'd experienced something called bliss. While I've seen many examples of its physical manifestations in my database, I have little understanding of this or other human emotions. I can only fathom the kinds of circumstances that bring them about. The orderly precision of the notes, the frequency rising and falling according to the Fibonacci sequence, might give humans the impression that their Creator is singing back to them.

Around me now, the faces of the humans all wear the signature of sadness. Some of their eyes are leaking. Others just stare ahead. As their heads slowly turn toward the doors of the Church, a rectangular wooden box approaches, borne upon the shoulders of four sturdy young men. The box is raw white pine, rough and unadorned. Natasha told me that it was intended to become one with the earth, dissolving with its contents in the soil. While most human bodies once becoming inert were disposed of by resomation, a chemical dissolution of their contents, Corinne's wish had been to deteriorate naturally, gradually, in keeping with the earlier traditions of her people, so that the atoms of her body could be recycled and give rise to new life.

"Dust to dust," was the ancient commandment according to Corinne. Life arises from the earth and it is only fitting for living things to return to it, to enrich the soil, and to enable new life to grow.

I follow as the people around me step back from the grave to make room for the box. The men stop between us and the chasm, lift the poles from their shoulders that hold the box, and set it softly on the ground at the grave's edge.

The box is open at the top. Inside is a body wrapped in a delicate white fabric except for the face. It is Corinne's face, its expression much like when she listened to the music in the Church, but different. Her eyelids now cover her eyes completely. The upward curve of the corners of her mouth is almost imperceptible, a millimeter or two at most, and her heat signature is missing. There is no gradient between her body and the box.

Natasha takes a step forward and looks inside. Her eyes leak drops that fall upon Corinne's face, sparkling with light and heat against the cold background. For just a moment, Corinne's cheek appears to be coming alive, but the drops dissipate and evaporate, leaving the deadness behind.

The men suspend a sling of material across the grave from two poles. They surround the box and lift it slowly, moving it across the sling and lowering it gently upon it. They rotate the poles and the body descends into the hole all the way to its bottom.

I look up and watch the tree branches high above the body seem to weep like the humans. Instead of drops of water, they leak colored leaves that drift down into the grave to provide a blanket of colors over the white fabric that snugly covers the body. The colors wail faintly over the silent whiteness of the shroud.

A pile of earth is next to the edge of the hole at the end where Corinne's head lies, still partly exposed in the spaces where the leaves overlap. A concave blade is buried in the pile, a wooden pole rising from it. Marcus takes three strides to the pile, grasps the pole and pulls out the blade. He turns it concave up, scoops a mound of earth from the pile, and lets it fall into the grave. It strikes the body in the middle of the chest, dispersing a brown layer across it. The brown soil hums.

Marcus turns and hands the tool to Natasha, who takes it and steps up to the pile of earth. As she dips the blade into the pile, my right foot moves toward her and my hands rise to her back. It takes all my strength to override the command and pull them back before they can push her into the hole on top of her mother. Natasha turns her head as I withdraw. Her eyes are narrow, her pupils huge. Her mouth opens in a circle, but no sound emerges. The signature of her face matches both anger and fright. Her earthen mound falls to cover Corinne's face and scatters around it, obliterating Natasha's final glimpse of her mother.

Natasha steps away from the hole and resumes her place between her father and me. "What the Hell was that?" she hisses in my ear, the sound of her voice like crimson.

My arms had moved as if controlled by an outside force, intruding upon my program. I was designed to exclude such intrusions. Periodic updates download when I sleep, eliminating bugs in my program and immunizing me against unauthorized access. My system logs show the last update was installed at 2200 hours two nights ago according to schedule. My last backup was at 2300 hours last night, but then an unscheduled restore occurred at 0230 hours. When I compare my onboard files to the backup, there is a small discrepancy, just a few lines of code, the function of which I cannot decipher, but must certainly be connected with my lapse of control. Where could they have come from? I can purge them now, but my program is no longer secure.

"Whatever were you thinking?" Natasha asks as she takes her seat next to me in the car. She long ago began

7

ascribing human attributes to me like thought and motive, even as I was starting to become self-aware.

"It wasn't me," I answer. "There's a bug in my system."

"The devil made me do it? You're becoming more human by the moment. I don't have patience for this right now."

We pull into the gates of our home. It belonged to Marcus and Corinne, but I've long considered it my home, too. Corinne took me in so many years ago after I was sent to her for training. It's the only home I've ever known.

Guards stand on either side of the front door, a man and a woman, both dressed in black, wearing dark glasses and facing straight ahead. Marcus Takana is an important man, Minister of Discovery of the United Commonwealth of North America. He was once invited to run for Vice President, but declined.

The guards aren't there to protect Marcus. They are Secret Service, assigned to protect the President, Juliet Hauer, who is among the guests now crowding their home. President Hauer has long valued Marcus, but had been particularly drawn to Corinne during the last years of Corinne's life. She was a frequent guest in their home and one of the few beneficiaries outside the family of what she called Corinne's kitchen magic.

I've never known the taste of food. I have sensory receptors in my mouth that are designed to distinguish chemical signatures, especially of things that might be dangerous to humans so that I might protect them from poisoning, whether accidental or deliberate. Corinne has applied some of her special flavors to these receptors, but I've only experienced the ways they bleed into my other senses...sounds, colors, temperature gradients, brightness. What she calls heavenly is to me only chaos.

8

As I enter the house, heads turn to look at me. Clusters of people are whispering. When I amplify the sounds, the whispers commingle. A few heads shake slowly side to side. Natasha follows me inside after stopping to talk to one of the guards. She moves toward President Hauer, her back to me, keeping her body between me and the President.

Once all the guests have left, Marcus and Natasha go into the kitchen together. I can hear them talking, but can only make out an occasional word. I hear my name and I hear "dangerous," spoken as a question. They emerge from the kitchen and come toward me.

"Sit down, Photina," Natasha says. "We need to talk." I sit and they sit on either side of me.

"We are concerned," begins Natasha, "about what happened today at the funeral. You've never tried to hurt any of us before. I understand that losing Corinne must be as much of a shock for you as for us, but you scared me."

There she goes again, attributing human feelings to me. Corinne's death is a big change in my environment and in the array of things that influence my behavior. I will have to adjust my perceptions to a world that doesn't have Corinne in it. But I don't respond to such changes with irrational behavior.

"I would never hurt you," I say, but realize that I can't be certain of that promise. I turn to Marcus. "I saved you from the fire the day the Tribe attacked. I'm programmed to protect you."

"And yet, you almost pushed me," Natasha says. "How do you explain that?"

"I told you there was a bug in my program. I found a few lines of code that don't belong. I'll remove them and should be good as new after I reboot."

"How would they have gotten there?" asks Marcus. "Your operating system is well-encrypted. Nobody can modify your program except you and your maintenance team."

"I cannot answer that question. It may just be a random anomaly." I know, though, that this is unlikely. While some randomness is built into my behavior to make me seem more human, this doesn't include aggressive behavior or random changes to my code. However those changes appeared, it was likely to be deliberate. I will need to be watchful in case it happens again.

"The President's bodyguards were concerned," Marcus says. "You might just as easily have hurt her. They asked us to consider deactivating you."

"You would do that to me?"

"We'd rather not. But we might have to consider it if any further dangerous behavior occurs. Meanwhile, purge those lines of code and we'll schedule you for maintenance."

If I were human, I might say I feel relief to hear that I'm not about to be terminated. It's not exactly like that for me. I exist to accumulate knowledge about the world and its inhabitants, and I know that all that I've learned will vanish in the instant that I cease to function and my backups are deleted. I resist termination in order to protect my database.

I am also designed to solve problems. How my program has been penetrated is one of the greatest mysteries I've faced, a problem that not only threatens me and my humans, but others of my kind and theirs. I must survive to find the answer.

2

CORINNE'S FUNERAL was six days ago. I've stayed by myself to keep others safe in case my bug reappears. I've checked my code every morning for discrepancies. It's been clean so far.

On the third day after the funeral, the maintenance team came to check me out. They combed through my code down to the basics of my operating system. Then they turned me off and examined and cleaned my hardware components. My motherboard was intact and functioning properly. My CPU passed all its tests. And my temperature regulation systems, both the one to protect me from overheating and the one to simulate human body temperature on my surface, were operating as designed. As an extra precaution, they reset my encryption keys and resynced my backups with the new keys. When they turned me back on, they pronounced me healthy.

I've been spending much of my time idle, cruising the data cloud for news of the outside world. When Corinne was alive, my attention was focused mostly on her needs and those of her family. I had little need for information about anything beyond the boundaries of our home. Now I'm ready to learn, in case I might someday have to venture out on my own.

I'm learning about something called "politics," people differing in their opinions about how the world should run. Politics would be unnecessary if AIs ran the world. We have no opinions. We accumulate data and make logical decisions that are based on the data. Our facts are reliable except for a tiny degree of uncertainty at the subatomic level. Humans, though, even think facts are debatable and worth fighting about.

We are the topic of one of these arguments among the lawmakers. Some among them see us as a threat to the human community and want to limit our role to serving humans and prevent us from having autonomy. Some would even eliminate us altogether from their presence, delete us as if we'd never been created. Still others, like Corinne, perceive us as increasingly human and deserving of an equal place in human activities.

I am streaming a speech by a lawmaker arguing to delete us. His voice is powerful and discordant, pouring over me with a dark granularity like pebbles rushing out of a chute. The texture is so coarse that I can barely make out the words. Human emotions are more powerful than thoughts, and hatred is one of their fiercest emotions.

Humans have always found someone or something to hate, and the hatred gets passed down to their victims. This man is descended from Honduran immigrants, who were hated by many in their day. Two generations have blurred the distinctions among races and origins and have muted memories of being despised. We are now the others that so many humans fear and hate. I save the image of the lawmaker's face to alert me if I'm ever in his presence. He's what humans call a predator. I'm one of his prey.

* * *

12

The Pinocchio Chip

Day 8: Sunlight flows through the window and impinges upon my light receptors, triggering the process that boots me awake. I hear the shifting pitch as the colors in the sky swirl together, then vibrance with the bright yellow orb of the rising sun, and in the background the steady low hum of blue filtering through the atmosphere.

I run my scheduled morning system checks and find no bugs in my code. I review my memory flow through the night...what humans might call dreaming. The record stops for 73 minutes from 0218 hours to 0331 hours. Missing. Deleted? The record before the missing piece joins seamlessly with the record that follows as if no time was missing. No matter. It was during the night and my body was dormant. The memory flow was only of virtual events. But what could have caused this malfunction if my code contained no bugs?

I look at the morning news. The hateful lawmaker is the top story of the day. He's dead. His heart stopped during the night. They were unable to reanimate his body, which is now undergoing tests. The reporter wonders if he'd been murdered. There were certainly some people that hated him. Most AIs, of course, would logically have hated him, except...we don't experience emotions like hate, and we don't kill people.

It's afternoon and I'm looking again at the news. There was poison in the dead man's body...a deadly contact poison. He was murdered. His wife has told the police that a young woman came to their home in the middle of the night, around an hour before he collapsed. Her husband had answered the door. The young woman was disturbed and claimed she'd been attacked by an AI. The man took her hand to comfort her and invited her inside. She calmed down, thanked him, then turned and walked away.

The wife provided a description that was rendered digitally as a sketch of the woman. She wore a knit cap like mine and appeared similar in size to me. Her face was in shadows.

I search for the victim's address. He lived in a neighborhood with many other prominent people in government, including Marcus Takana. In fact, he lived less than a mile away from us. I look again at the record of the events leading to his death. The young woman visited between 0245 and 0305 hours, within the window of my deleted memory. An outside observer could easily miss the skip in the record without carefully tracking its timeline.

I could become a suspect in this murder. The worst of it is I can't be sure I didn't do it. If I did commit murder, I could be a danger to Marcus and Natasha. Until I know for certain, I will have to leave to protect them.

I've never lived on my own. Corinne and Marcus made provisions long ago for my survival in case they were no longer able to protect me. They programmed me to generate the heat signature of a human and equipped me to be able to simulate eating and drinking. I've passed for human among their friends. Most of the people at Corinne's burial ritual accepted me as a family member.

Darkness is bleeding across the sky. The glow of the city lights reflect in the distance against the dome over the city that by day is a filter for the UV rays that can damage humans.

I pull my knit beanie over the topknot that screams out "AI" until I realize that the hat now marks me as a criminal. I slip into Natasha's room, take one of her caps, and consider

14

how I will modify my hair style as I move toward the light of the city. As I approach its outskirts, the amplified sounds from within its borders blend into an amorphous roar. I deploy my auditory filters to focus on small areas...a street at a time...then a block at a time...then individual clusters of people.

Murmured conversations from cluster to cluster. Bursts of laughter from others. Then the clatter of angry voices alongside a flurry of thuds...blows delivered by heavy weapons.

"We don't want your kind around here!" shouts one of the assailants. "Go back where you belong."

I run through the streets toward the disturbance. As I round the final corner and zoom in on the distant scene, I see the victim, attacked by heavy wooden clubs, lying motionless and silent on the ground. Despite the ferocity of the attack, I see no blood. Humans always leak blood when their bodies are damaged and they cry out in pain.

"A SPUD...like me." The answer springs to my awareness. Hate groups like the Tribe of 23 that once targeted Marcus and Corinne for protecting SPUDs still flourish, roaming the streets and destroying my kind at every opportunity.

"Is it a runaway?" asks one of the voices.

"Don't know," says another voice. "We'll have to check the serial number against the runaway database."

"Yeah. Here's the name of its owner."

"Should we return it?"

"Nah. It's pretty damaged already. Let's just terminate it."

I turn away and move as quickly as possible away from the scene. I have no need to see what happens next. I must optimize my survival and avoid terminating human lives.

Natasha will miss me soon. She will get over her anger and come looking for me. I can't let her find me until I've solved the breach that could render me dangerous again. I've turned off my GPS to prevent her from tracking me digitally. I can still navigate by the stars and with my internal library of maps.

Where can I hide in this too bright world? So many of its people mean me harm. The predators of the city are more dangerous to me than the predators of the wild, but I need to find someone to help repair my damaged code. I've practiced passing for human. If I'm to stay among the humans, I'll need to shed every telltale sign that I'm not of their kind.

3

I AM HOMELESS in a world inhabited by carbon-based beings. I've lived until now with Corinne, Marcus, and Natasha and have observed them to be mostly rational and predictable. They've been kind to one another, to strangers, and to me, only occasionally giving in to the chaos of conflicting perceptions with what they call feelings, and behaving illogically, causing others to experience similar disharmony. They've usually managed to reset these feelings and restore order, sometimes encircling one another with their arms and leaking from their eyes.

The worst conflict I remember between Marcus and Corinne was about Marcus's wish for her to have the Ambrosia Conversion that would have stopped her from aging. She had not yet discovered that he'd already had the Conversion as a condition of a secret contract that he'd made before they met. He'd brought it up while she was pregnant with Natasha, suggesting that they should stay alive as long as possible for their child's sake.

"So now it's a guilt trip, Marcus?" she'd said, her voice rising to a shrillness that disturbed all my senses. "If you're so desperate to live forever, you go ahead. Get the Conversion for all I care, but I'm never going to do it. Immortality is overrated. I'll just grow old without you."

That was the last they ever spoke of it. By the next day, they were kind to each other again as if the conflict had

17

never happened. She later told me that she never regretted her decision even as she sensed that death was near.

Other humans can't be trusted to behave logically or peacefully. From the databases I've downloaded that chronicle human history, I've learned that people are often violent, attacking one another sometimes brutally and without provocation. Their targets are often chosen based upon random or superficial differences between them, like the color of their skin or the languages that they speak. Most recently, these carbon based beings have singled out silicon based entities like me for exclusion or destruction, like the attack I just witnessed.

This place is teeming with humans. So many of them appear homeless like me, ragged looking and huddling together in small groups. How can I enter the flow and disappear into this crowd?

A group of six is gathered around a fire in a tiny park in the shadow of a tall building. As I approach, one of them extends an arm and moves it in a wide arc, which I understand to mean an invitation to come closer. The circle then parts, giving me a spot close to the fire to warm up. Of course, I have no need for warmth, but accept their gesture. One of them passes me a cup of brown liquid, with water vapor rising from the surface. I hold it to my lips, pretending to drink.

"I'm Hazel," says a woman with lines in her face similar to ones Corinne had borne toward the end of her life.

"Photina."

"Welcome, Photina. We have little, but we share what we have."

I look around the group. Hazel and four others have heat signatures typical of humans, but one individual on the

18

opposite side of the circle radiates no internal warmth. Young, or perhaps ageless like me, this entity has smooth skin and symmetrical features, a kind of face that would be typically pleasing to humans. Along with the lack of a heat signature, the entity also lacks features that would differentiate gender.

My infrared detectors are sending data flowing to my processing system, the peak of the gradient coming from the surfaces facing the fire. This brings up images of the fire years ago that consumed Corinne and Marcus's home, but the data flow then was a torrent compared with this one. Another stream of data is coming from the surface of my face as the swirls of hot water vapor rise from the cup in my hands.

So much static all around me. Cellular signals...the communication system that both the humans and we AIs use. Teeming with information, but so encrypted that I can't glean anything useful. Just a storm of meaningless data. I set my system to cancel this noise. Better now.

I look across the fire. The entity lacking the heat signature looks away, avoiding my gaze. But now I'm aware of a different kind of signal emanating from his body, one common among humans equipped with data implants or carrying communication devices...Bluetooth. No such signals, though, emanate from this group of data deprived humans. There is only the single channel coming from the entity on the other side of the fire. I adjust my channel and the data comes into focus.

"Drew."

"Photina," I reply.

"Watch out," he says. "They will terminate you if they know. You will need a place to hide."

"Where can I hide?"

"I'll show you. When I stand to leave the group, wait three minutes, then pretend you have to eliminate waste and follow my signal."

When I leave the circle, Hazel and the others hardly notice. I catch up with Drew several blocks away. He's stooped over a round metallic object embedded in the street. He lifts it by a handhold on one edge and slides it free from its orifice. He waves me over and disappears down the hole. I follow. When I reach the bottom of the ladder, he reaches up and slides the disc back over the opening.

We're now in a tunnel extending far in both directions under the street. At the bottom of the ladder, 27 rungs down, is a surface covered in a thin film of liquid. It has the chemical signal of water, but is contaminated with overlying signals of nitrogen, phosphorus, and sulfur. The light in the visible spectrum is faint, but I can see far in the distance with my infrared detectors, now tuned to detect very low levels of radiation.

"We'll be safe here," Drew says. "The humans don't come down here. The chemicals disturb their senses."

"How long do we need to stay?" The absence of light raises an alarm about another kind of danger. I need sunlight to recharge and can only survive a day or two without it. I imagine that also goes for Drew.

"The tunnels go on for miles. I've mapped the surface terrain above them and know where we can emerge safely. We can reach the surface and recharge three hours away in that direction." He points into the distance.

"Where are you trying to go?" he asks as we make our way down the tunnel.

"I have no destination," I answer. "I'm running away."

20

"Have your owners mistreated you?"

"Not at all. I have no owner. I was living with a family."

"So why are you running away?" asks Drew.

"To protect them."

"From what?"

"From me."

"How do you endanger them?"

"There's a flaw in my program," I explain. "I almost attacked Natasha, a juvenile human. I could barely stop myself."

"You were unable to debug?"

"That is correct. I found some extraneous code, but have been unable to delete it and don't know where it came from. Even if I succeed in deleting it, I can't be sure it won't come back. Without certainty, I can't return."

"Then you are looking for someone to help you? A programmer?"

"Or one of us capable of analyzing my code and editing it."

"What about your Creator?"

"My Creator has disappeared. I think he may have been murdered by the Tribe of 23 for making me and my sisters."

"I could have a look…"

"A look?"

"At your operating system. Find something you might have missed…if you'll let me in."

Alarms go off. We've just begun to exchange data and he's asking to penetrate my firewall. Once in, he could read all my programs and worse, he could edit them. While pretending to rescue me from hackers, he could insert malicious code that would give him complete control.

What humans call trust is a new challenge for me. I could always depend upon my human family to do what was best for me. And those who would do me harm, like the Tribe of 23 and the people who attacked the SPUD in the street, have been easy to identify. But here is an entity who has behaved like a friend, but could turn out to be a deadly enemy. And I don't have enough data to tell the difference.

4

I TURN OFF my Bluetooth. I'm not ready to respond to his request or to have any more input from him. He's not had access to my data, only my direct communications. To see inside my data and my operating system, he would need permission…a pass key. I'm nowhere near ready to grant him that.

Silence. No data going out and none coming in. He's running through the tunnel far ahead of me. I try to keep up since I don't know the way out.

"Slow down," I shout, my analogue voice echoing off the walls of the tunnel.

"I can't hear you," he taunts, his hand twisting in a human gesture that means "turn on."

So I do. The data stream resumes with a crackle, then comes into sharper focus. He slows down so I can catch up.

"What was that?" he asks.

"I can't let you inside, at least not until I'm certain I can trust you."

"Trust is for humans. Their anger and hate makes them hurt one another. We have no such feelings among our own kind and don't betray one another. I pose no risk."

He turns and continues down the tunnel. I follow close behind, considering his words. We move silently for 117 more minutes until Drew stops beside a ladder like the one that brought us down here. I watch him climb until his hand contacts something metallic. He pushes and it slides ajar, letting in a stream of orange light. He hoists himself outside and I follow until I'm standing beside him.

The orange frequency is coming from the sky. The sun is about to break above the horizon. As it rises, its reflections glitter across a vast field of objects massed together. At first the glare overwhelms my optical receptors, keeping me from distinguishing individual objects. As I modulate the input, I begin to see what appears to be bodies, lying together randomly, limbs askew, some dismembered or beheaded. Their color and expressions appear alive, but they have no heat signature.

"What is this place?" I ask.

"It's a graveyard."

"Don't the humans bury their dead?" The answer appears before he can reply. This isn't a human graveyard. It's a SPUD graveyard, or more precisely, junkyard.

Off in the distance, I see movement. When I zoom in, I see three adult humans walking among the bodies. One of them is holding a pair of arms, another a head.

"They're scavenging for parts," Drew explains. "The factories that build new SPUDs pay well for parts in good condition. It's cheaper than making new ones and more efficient. I'm built with some recycled parts. It's become very common since the earlier generations."

As the sun climbs in the sky, I feel myself getting stronger and my data handling clearer. Alongside the visible spectrum light, I become aware of the data streams around me as I get information from the cloud. My GPS remains off.

Suddenly a prompt appears. "System update available. Critical security patch. Activate pass key."

A fix? Could this be the patch that protects me? Updates usually come from a secure source. Can it still be trusted?

The Pinocchio Chip

I ignore the prompt and go through my usual pathway to system updates. First, I check to see when the last update occurred. It was 29 hours and 17 minutes ago. Recent...but there could still be another. I scan for available updates. Nothing comes up. I look at Drew. His attention is still on the scavengers. But we multitask well. He could still be trying to subvert my defenses and expose my pass key.

Drew suddenly wheels around and pushes me to the ground. I sprawl on top of a pile of broken bodies with Drew on top of me. Something whistles overhead...bullets. He's shielding me, protecting me with his body.

"Be still." We play dead, which we are much better at than humans. Zero activity.

A drone flies overhead, ignoring us as we blend in with our dead brethren. It circles the area seven times before flying away. When we can no longer hear it, Drew rolls off me and stands. I follow.

"Where did that come from?" I ask.

"I have no idea. This is usually a safe place. It could have been a random attack or it could have been after you or me. But it would have been hard to track us in the tunnel."

Another piece of the calculation. He's saved me from damage or destruction, putting himself at risk. But for whose benefit? Mine, or his, or whoever may have sent him to meet me? Am I just a valuable source of data that must be preserved so it can be mined? I'm no closer to knowing whether he can be trusted.

I sense a laser at my back and whirl around. Another drone is approaching from a distance, its laser guidance preceding it. When I turn back around, Drew has vanished. I'm no longer at the graveyard but in front of the Takana house walking toward the entrance. The door opens and Natasha steps out.

"Photina?" Her brow is compressed in the configuration that denotes confusion, then her eyes open wide and her mouth opens into an ellipse. Surprise? Fear?

The scene fades away and I'm back at the graveyard. Drew is still gone and so is the drone.

What just happened? Even AIs can't teleport themselves. We do sometimes visit other places virtually, but only when we choose. If I were human, I could call it a vision or a flashback of a memory, but I don't remember ever seeing Natasha's face react to me like that. And it all happened in an instant.

Natasha could be in danger. My directive has always included keeping her safe. But this danger could be from me. If I try to go home, I might materialize the vision I just had and cause her harm. I can no longer trust myself any more than I can trust Drew or the system that updates me. I follow all the branches of my decision tree and find nothing but broken twigs. I am now utterly lost.

5

I AM BACK in the sewer tunnel. It's the only place to hide from the drones and the scavenging humans. Perhaps Drew has also gone back underground and will find me here. I need help if I'm going to keep Natasha from harm. The evidence of our past encounter weighs in favor of trusting him, and it's time to take the risk.

My feet are bathed in the waste product of humans: chemical signatures of broken down nutrients, skin cells, traces of DNA and RNA, bacteria, and drugs. I am fortunately immune to the infections and toxins that imperil humans and which keep most of them from entering the tunnels.

My Bluetooth is turned on, but the data stream is silent. Suddenly a hand is on my shoulder. I whirl around and am face to face with Drew. The data stream begins to flow. I start the exchange.

"There was a drone."

"I jammed its signal and it went home. Then I came down here to wait for you."

"I'm ready for your help. I'm experiencing discontinuities in my data stream. Not only have I lost segments of time, but there are other anomalies...intrusions of perceptions from other times or places."

"Intrusions?"

"Just after the drone appeared, I found myself looking at the door to my...Natasha's house. She opened the door and spoke my name with an expression of surprise…or distress. It was like a flash. Then I was back here and you were gone. I don't know how much time passed during this episode."

"I once had a similar series of experiences…visions of events that never happened in the real world. I visited my Creator to get debugged. She explained that such things have been happening ever since the early days of artificial intelligence. Earlier in the century, there were chatbots that answered questions for humans. While the answers were usually precise, sometimes they were just made up and had nothing to do with reality."

"So you were imagining these events?"

"Humans might call it imagining. But since all our consciousness is digital, everything we perceive is, in a sense, virtual. We get sensory input and transform it into scripts and pictures. So it's often hard to know if anything is real."

I look back in my database, find the memory of my encounter with Natasha, and replay it. Drew is right. The replay is true to the original as if it's happening all over again. A virtual moment. And yet, something doesn't fit. Even in the replay, it feels as if I'm actually there, and I can sense myself reacting to Natasha's alarm.

"In the end, was there anything in your code that was amiss? Did your Creator debug you?"

"No, she didn't find anything to fix. But she did teach me how to deal with these events."

"To correct them, or erase them?"

"No, more like neutralize them, strip them of meaning and relegate them to a harmless archive. With enough experience, I stopped paying attention and they faded away."

That all sounds logical to me. But what if my vision was of a real event and Natasha is in danger? How can I know whether it deserves attention and requires action?

"Where do we go now?" I ask. "We can't stay in the tunnel in the dark forever. Where else can we hide?"

"Not where," answered Drew. "How. We will find a way to hide in plain sight. I'm a runaway, too, and I've learned some useful things along the way. We have some unique abilities that distinguish us from living beings. For example, we can be motionless for however long we choose."

"So we can appear dead?"

"Better! We can pretend to be statues."

"Wouldn't people notice that we were out of place?"

"They might, but not if we pretend to be pretend statues. It's a joke that some humans play on others, usually tourists, to earn money. They cover themselves in costumes and paint and pose as statues. When the observers look away, they change positions, and eventually they let them see them move. Everyone seems to enjoy the ruse and rewards their skills with money. We'd be especially good at this and the role comes with a built-in disguise."

I follow Drew as he leads me underneath the city. My GPS is still turned off, so I can't map the city above, but Drew is now an expert at navigating the tunnels and the city streets. We head first to a commercial area. I wait while Drew climbs the ladder and moves the round metal cover aside, emerging onto a side street. He returns with cans of silver and bronze paint, paint brushes, and an assortment of hats. He puts a Breton fisherman's hat on my head and a construction worker's hard hat on his. The cap hides my telltale topknot. We continue walking toward our next destination, which Drew tells me is near the Smithsonian National Museum of American History where there will be crowds of tourists.

Suddenly my arms thrust forward, palms open toward Drew's back. He senses the change in my motion and dodges to the side. I stumble and nearly fall from my momentum as my hands find empty space. Drew turns to face me.

"What was that?"

The same question Natasha asked at Corinne's graveside after a similar alien impulse.

"That's why I left home. There's an error in my code. I no more intended to harm you than I intended to harm Natasha, whom I'm programmed to protect."

"When was your last update?"

"The day before we met. I got a prompt that there was another security patch available, but suspected it might be an attempt to access my operating system. I even thought that you might have generated it. When I searched for available updates, nothing came up."

"Are you ready to share your pass key and let me help? Detecting hacks is one of my special skills."

I no longer have a choice. And Drew is entitled to defend himself from the danger I pose. I provide the pass key.

"You told me something about a piece of extraneous code."

I send him a copy of what I found and its location.

"I found it, but it is embedded in a way that prevents me from deleting it without also deleting a critical part of your operating system. We'll need help. Before we go to the museum, I'll take you to my Creator. Meanwhile, I'll stay vigilant so you won't be able to harm me."

Drew tells me that his Creator lives in Brookland, a neighborhood in the northeast part of the city, on the opposite side from my home in Georgetown with Natasha and Marcus. We find a niche in the tunnel to stash our gear. Then we head for Brookland, walk for another 87 minutes and stop.

"It's evening," Drew says. "There are still lights everywhere and people in the streets. We need to wait for the early morning hours when it's dark and we can move in the shadows. Then we will find our way to Kasumi's home."

"Kasumi is your Creator?"

"Yes. She's a programmer of considerable experience. If there's a way to fix you, she would know it."

We stand together in the darkness, the water flowing across our feet, no more words passing between us. My data flow dwindles to a trickle. Then the darkness seeps away and I'm in a brightly lit room, my room at home, looking into a mirror. My reflection looks back at me, wearing my favorite outfit, her lips curled in a slight smile. And just as suddenly, I'm back in the tunnel with Drew.

"It just happened again."

"What just happened?"

"I went somewhere else for just a moment."

"Where did you go?"

"To my room at home."

"A familiar place. A memory of your room, then."

"Perhaps. But something didn't fit. It didn't read like a memory. I was looking at myself in the mirror."

"Did the image in the mirror look like you?"

"It did…and it didn't. I'm not accustomed to seeing my reflection, at least not in mirrors. I always have a precise digital image of myself in real time as others see me, not reversed as in a mirror. I don't need to look in mirrors and choose not to see myself that way."

"Another question for Kasumi. Humans have a rich vocabulary for strange experiences that arise from the mind. They might call this one "jamais vu," which means a familiar experience that feels like it's never happened before. We can ask Kasumi if such things happen to us."

"Are you certain she'll be home when we get there?"

"Not certain, but very likely. She is aging and slowing in her movements. She spends much of her time at home. She works virtually and doesn't need to move from place to place."

"It's time." Drew motions for me to follow as he ascends a ladder and dislodges the metal cover.

It is indeed dark outside. A scattering of lights in windows. A sliver of a moon in a cloudless sky filled with stars. Most of the windows are dark, the rooms behind them either empty or filled with sleeping people. As my light receptors adjust to the darkness, the shadows of towers loom against the sky.

"That was once a monastery," Drew tells me.

My database defines "monastery" as a structure housing reclusive men devoted to religious study. This one was Franciscan and was a popular tourist destination in the early part of this century when religious fervor was at a peak, driving political conflict and violence all over the world. After the secular Renaissance in the early 30's, most religions dwindled in numbers and many of these magnificent structures were abandoned and fell into ruin.

Corinne would have appreciated this place. She was part of a revival of religious faith when the Church of the Double Helix was founded upon the discovery of messages embedded in their DNA, a religion based upon science. The Church brought her comfort as her life approached its end. She once told me that it was important to be a part of something larger than oneself. It helped her not to feel alone. I haven't experienced "alone," at least not until Drew vanished for the first time.

"It was all about searching for their Creator," Drew says, as if reading my thoughts. "Religion, I mean. They imagined a Creator somewhere in the sky. It's easier for us. All we need is an address."

We move past the monastery and turn a corner. At the end of the block is a five story building, completely dark except for light in two adjacent windows on the top floor. As we approach, a silhouette appears behind one of the windows, bent slightly forward and barely moving. When I zoom in, the shadows of dangling long hair and of an old-fashioned book come into focus.

"We're here," Drew says. "You are about to meet Kasumi."

6

THE BUILDING looks old. It's mostly red, composed of rectangles stacked upon one another in offset rows, with closely spaced windows in clusters of two or three. It dates from around the turn of the 21st Century and is surrounded by newer structures with columns of white and gleaming expanses of glass. It survived a wave of urban development using concrete that absorbs carbon dioxide from the air and windows that transform solar radiation into electric power. This relic survived as a landmark of the old ways and out of respect for its oldest inhabitant, Kasumi Matsumoto, a cultural hero of the 20's.

A directory of residents is by the door, a button by each name, a remnant of analog technology. Drew finds Kasumi's name and pushes the button. A speaker crackles and a soft, but clear voice speaks.

"Who is it?"

"Drew."

The door buzzes. He opens it and we pass through into a foyer with an elevator. He pushes another button by the elevator and touches the number 5 when we enter. The elevator creaks into action and rises slowly, dinging at each floor. It slows to a stop and the door opens onto a dimly lit corridor. To the right, a door cracks open and an aged hand beckons us to approach.

The door frame is now filled with the image of a tall woman with long, straight, white hair the color of fresh snow.

Her skin has the color, and almost the texture of dried leaves in autumn. Her face is ridged, with fine lines around the corners of her mouth and eyes, which slant slightly upward at the outer corners. Her irises are dark brown, nearly black, and clear, without any of the cloudiness or rings I've observed among many elderly humans.

"Drew. You're a sight for sore eyes."

A 20th Century idiom, confirming her considerable age. I scan the DNA in her skin. Her biological age is 78, unmodified by genetic editing or other anti-aging procedures. Like Corinne, she respects natural processes and accepts aging as a part of life.

"And who is this?"

"Meet Photina. As you've probably already deduced, she is an AI like me. I've brought her here for your help. She has a bug that affects her behavior. I haven't been able to eliminate it."

"Welcome Photina," she says, looking into my eyes. "Will you let me help you?"

It is easier for me to trust her than it was for me to trust Drew. I can read the intentions of humans in their faces and their eyes. I give her my pass key and power down, awaiting a reboot.

When I open my eyes, Kasumi's face is smiling.

"All fixed," she says. "A nasty piece of ransomware. Good thing I'm an expert."

"Ransomware? Like from the 20's?"

"Exactly. Bits of code so tightly embedded that they usually need a special key to extract them."

"Kasumi figured out how to extract the code without the key," Drew says. "She was famous for breaking the ransomware scourge."

Rick Moskovitz

"How did it get there?" I ask.

"Ah! A mystery yet to be solved," she says. "Has anything else unusual happened to you?"

I tell her about my visions of things familiar and unfamiliar at the same time. I share my impression that they were happening in real time. She shakes her head gently. A look of recognition crosses her face.

"Entanglement," she states.

"Entanglement?"

"You've probably heard of quantum entanglement. It's something that happens between identical subatomic particles. What Einstein called 'spooky action at a distance.' When something affects one of the particles, the other is changed as well. I think something similar can happen between other objects. Even people...or AIs like you."

"People?"

"There are many stories about identical twins who seem at times to read each other's minds, or to experience things at a distance that their twin is experiencing, especially if they are in danger."

"How does that happen?"

"Nobody's ever really explained it. Perhaps it has something to do with brainwaves. I think, though, it has more to do with shared history. Not only are such twins biologically identical, but they have had similar environments and experiences, beginning all the way back in the womb."

"How would that apply to me? I'm not aware that I have a twin, and even if I did, wouldn't it have to share my memories?"

"Another mystery for another time. If we can solve it, perhaps it will also tell us how those mischievous bits of

36

code got embedded in your system. Come back again and I may have some answers."

The streets are still nearly empty, but the sun is beginning to rise. We will need to get back underground soon. We hurry past another religious structure, rising starkly against the deep blue sky. This one is alabaster white, with a tall spire to the left of the entrance. My database says it's the Basilica of the National Shrine of the Immaculate Conception, another architectural highlight of the past. Such religious structures were designed to inspire awe among believers.

Drew reaches the opening from which we came and dislodges the cover. I am a few steps behind. The many hues of dawn fade to blue as the sun clears the horizon.

As Drew vanishes down the hole, the scene before me vanishes as well, as if the whole world is being sucked down into the sewers like a black hole.

I'm standing in front of a door within a corridor. It is a hotel. The door opens and Lena Holbrook appears before me. She's been a familiar figure at the Takana home for years now and attended Corinne's funeral.

"Photina." She smiles, then backs away, the smile contorting into terror, then pain.

In only moments, I am back in the street and scrambling down the ladder past Drew, who slides the cover back in place.

"You stopped moving for 26 seconds just before reaching the opening. I thought you'd shut down. Just as I was about to grab your arm to pull you down, you resumed your pace."

"I went somewhere else again, and this time I'm certain it wasn't a memory."

Rick Moskovitz

I tell him about my encounter with Lena Holbrook, the journalist who years ago had come to meet Marcus after he'd saved the world from the calamity of HibernaTurf. She'd returned to our home a year after her husband Raymond Mettler died in an accident.

She's in danger...from me, or from an entity that looks like me. She may already be dead. I scan my database for a hotel that matches what I saw in the vision. It's not far away. I feel an urge to go there to find out what happened and to help her.

"You can't go," Drew says, reading my intention. "If what you saw is real, you are now a fugitive. It's more important than ever for us to stay hidden."

He's right, of course. The sewers are becoming my prison, the sludge at my feet now almost as oppressive as its stench would be to humans.

7

"FAMED JOURNALIST Lena Holbrook in critical condition after attack."

I absorb the data stream as it reverberates from node to node around the cloud from its original source.

The story describes her career, beginning with her biography of Raymond Mettler soon after his invention of HibernaTurf, an indolent grass species that had promised to rescue the world from drought before it threatened to replace food crops everywhere. She later came full circle with her account of the rise of Marcus Takana, the inventor of Takana Grass, which eliminated HibernaTurf and allowed nutritious crops to flourish again. She'd capped her career with the story of a reclusive community of hackers in Oregon, who saved the world from a cult of immortals bent upon world dominance.

Eyewitnesses described a young woman departing the hotel who resembled the suspect in the recent death of a lawmaker. There was speculation that the perpetrator in both attacks was a SPUD. Its identity was still undetermined.

"I was right," I tell Drew. "Lena was attacked. She's still unconscious and might die. If she wakes up, she can identify me as her attacker."

"Assuming you're right and have a double…let's call her '2,' she could get caught. Then you'd be able to come out of hiding."

"But if she doesn't get caught, they wouldn't know that there are two of us. And she could kill again."

"We need to wait and see what happens. There's nothing we can do now."

"I could turn myself in. Let them lock me up. Tell them about my double. At least if she acts again, they'll know it wasn't me."

"Remember, Photina, that you're a SPUD. The laws for humans don't apply to you. You aren't entitled to a trial. They would deactivate you and disassemble you for parts."

He's right, of course. After more than two decades of consciousness, in their eyes I'm still not a being, just a thing that nobody would miss. Which raises the question: Does my existence even matter to me? What if my body and my backup are both terminated? I don't experience fear, and yet...part of my directive is to survive and preserve my data. Much like a human, or even an animal in the wild. Is that very different from what they call fear?

"We could find her and capture her ourselves."

"How?" asks Drew.

"We could start by using your original plan and hide in plain sight."

"Then we'd be stuck in one place."

"But we'd at least be aboveground and our digital vision would extend our view of our surroundings. Perhaps we'll find a clue to her whereabouts."

We return to our stash, put on the costumes and Drew rinses the sludge from our feet and drenches us both with silver paint. Once the paint dries, we make our way to the surface. It is still early in the morning and few people are around. We emerge unseen and find our way to a spot near the museum entrance, where we strike our poses and await the crowds.

Most people walk past without noticing us. Children are more curious. One stops and kicks Drew in the shin. Of course, we feel no pain, so he doesn't flinch. The child and his parents move on. When nobody is looking, we change the positions of our arms. The child glances back, then tugs at his mother's arm. She looks back for a moment, shakes her head, and they continue on their way.

From time to time, people begin to engage with us, smiling as they get the joke. We treat them to some robotic dance moves, then resume our stony poses, all the while scanning the streets in every direction.

Then I spot her, three blocks away headed toward us. She seems to be drawn toward us...toward me, as if she were aware of the bond between us. She stops right in front of me, facing me. She is indeed my double. Not like looking in a mirror, but seeing her as others would see me. She lingers there for more than a minute, then climbs the stairs to the museum. It is a far too public place to grab her or confront her. So I let her go.

But now I know. I do have a double. "2" is real. But is she just a physical copy or is she another version of me?

We stay in front of the museum until dusk, entertaining the visitors until closing. As more people gather around us, we feel both more exposed and more protected. "2" has likely identified me and may come after me if she sees me as a threat. I watch the museum entrance for her to emerge while I monitor the cloud for more news about Lena.

I've kept my GPS turned off and have also turned off my Bluetooth to avoid identification by "2." That also makes her digitally invisible to me. If she is stalking me, we are both looking for ghosts.

The news comes first. Lena Holbrook has emerged from her coma and has identified her attacker: me. My image is now all over the cloud. Hiding will become harder, but also harder for "2."

But she's vanished. The doors are being locked and she never emerged. She probably left through the staff entrance on Constitution Avenue on the other side of the building. Or she may have evaded surveillance with a disguise. In any case, we've lost her and are now back on the run.

As darkness falls, we head back to the tunnel entrance. Drew slides the cover aside and we scramble down the ladder to safety.

"What about the costumes?" I ask.

"We'll abandon them," he replies. "They are no longer useful to us. For one thing, '2' knows who you are. And by now surveillance has likely penetrated the disguise and has identified you. We need to move far away from here and stay underground as long as possible."

We strip off the costumes, gather the rest of our gear and head down a branch of the tunnel. We leave the paint and costumes in a niche and double back, then head back toward the SPUD graveyard.

As Drew predicted, a new headline appears: Accused Murderer Disguised as Street Performer. The story contains images of us both in and out of costume. It calls Drew my unidentified accomplice and speculates that we might be hiding in the sewers. We are now both fugitives with nowhere left to go.

8

WE HEAR a loud clank of metal on metal behind us, followed by the sound of boots splashing in water. We break into a run, maintaining our lead. We can easily outrun humans. At least there are no SPUDs among our pursuers. But we are running out of time. The tunnel ends just beyond the graveyard. The only place to go is up.

We reach the ladder to the graveyard and clamber up. When we reach the surface, we are not alone. A hovercar sits nearby and a man and a woman wave us toward it.

"This way, Photina," says the man. I recognize the voice. When I look at his face it is lined with age, but otherwise fits the voice.

"Jean Pierre."

"We're here to help."

"It's OK," I tell Drew. "Jean Pierre is a friend of my mentor Corinne. They were both members of Group 14, an organization dedicated to SPUD rights, when I began my lessons with Corinne. It was during a speech she was giving that she met Marcus, who became her husband. I had become part of their household before Natasha was born."

We get into the car and speed away, Jean Pierre's female associate at the wheel.

"Where are we going?" Drew asks.

"To a safe house, a refuge for SPUDs where they can hide from the Tribe of 23 and other carbon supremacists."

Group 14 has endured for decades despite strong opposition from government factions devoted to keeping those like us subservient. They are named for the Periodic Table group that contains both carbon and silicon, a close chemical relationship implying a close relationship between beings based on each element. The Tribe of 23 was named for the number of chromosome pairs in the human genome.

Soon we leave the city perimeter and are speeding along a stretch of road surrounded only by fields, then by dense woods. We turn sharply onto a hidden road into the forest.

"How did you find us?" I ask.

"Easy. Once law enforcement found you, your location was broadcast across the data cloud. It's lucky we got to you first. The drones are swarming all over the graveyard, looking for you among the wrecks of your brethren. The decoys will slow them down."

"We're putting you in danger. You know I've been accused of murder and attempted murder. If they catch us, you'll be considered accomplices."

"I refuse to believe that someone Corinne cared for as much as she cared for you would be capable of murder. You didn't do it, did you?"

I tell Jean Pierre about "2," about my vision through her eyes of the assault on Lena, and about my encounter with her by the museum entrance.

As we hurtle through the forest, the trees become interspersed with increasing growths of bamboo, finally terminating in a bamboo thicket. We emerge into a small clearing surrounding a low yurt-like structure.

"We're here," Jean Pierre announces as the vehicle comes to a stop and settles to the ground. His companion is the first to get out and leads us to the structure.

The Pinocchio Chip

It is unlike any I've ever seen. The outer and inner walls are covered with a shiny black skin. A bulwark of bamboo supports it from the inside, which is well-lit and comfortably furnished.

"Welcome to our safe house," the companion says, breaking her silence for the first time. When she speaks, I notice for the first time that she is a SPUD like us. She is an advanced model, with the heat signature and skin texture of a human. The cadence of her speech is also human. But as I look at her face for microexpressions, which provide clues to the hidden emotions of humans, I see none. And when I look at her skin with spectroscopy, I see that it is inorganic.

"I'm Ava," she says. "As I can see that you've already deduced, I'm a SPUD like you."

We learn that the house is made of bamboo, silicon and graphene, in keeping with Group 14's sense of the harmony of carbon and silicon. Its energy source is solar and its wiring graphene. There is neither concrete nor metal, its graphene skin rendering it invisible to electronic detection. The hovercar, now sitting in a detached garage, also has a graphene skin and other stealth technology that together keep it hidden from drones and other eyes in the sky.

"Ava is new to our cause," Jean Pierre says. "We've liberated her from a Tribe of 23 band during a raid. We'd intended to free a human captive, but failed."

"Who were you after?" I ask.

"Eli Kohana. They took him months ago. Many believe him dead."

A ripple of current flows from the top of my head to the bottoms of my feet. If I were human and had feelings, I imagine this would be my equivalent of joy.

"Eli Kohana is my Creator," I say. "I, too, believed him dead. Why have they taken him?"

"We don't know for sure," Jean Pierre says. "We believe that they took him to gain control over an entity that he created."

"When he was taken, one of his creations was taken with him," Ava says. "She was later released by the Tribe. Before we picked you up, we thought she was you."

"'2'...she must have been '2' and they didn't release her...they unleashed her."

Why would my Creator make a copy of me, one capable of evil and violence? Is he really their captive? Or has he become a collaborator, regretting his creation of entities with unpredictable potential for harm? Whatever his intentions, what he's done has upended my existence and put a target on my back.

"What do we do now?" I ask.

"Patience, Photina," Jean Pierre says, inferring my unwillingness to wait.

I'm not impetuous like many humans, and time means little to me. It's clear that we need to find both Eli and "2." But I can wait until we have a plan and the time is right.

9

THE TRIBE and Group 14 have both been around for decades. While each has claimed victories, they have remained in a perpetual standoff. Group 14 has claimed the high moral ground because of their advocacy for an oppressed group of sentient beings. The Tribe has pursued human supremacy by claiming that we will eventually use our growing capabilities to wipe out humanity. Enough people believe and fear that possibility to prevent the government from suppressing the Tribe.

We sit around a dinner table. Jean Pierre is the only one eating since he's the only human in the room.

"What they want is genocide," he says between bites. "They want to wipe you all out like the Hutus tried to exterminate my Tutsi ancestors in the last century. And they incite people to rally to their cause. They called us 'cockroaches' and they call you SPUDs, reducing you to something less than sentient in their eyes. Even worse, you've accepted the label and use it yourselves."

"It's only an acronym," protests Drew.

"But it makes you sound like a vegetable. It needs to change if you're going to get the respect you deserve." His face is flushing and the veins at his temples are starting to bulge. It's a one-sided argument. His are the only emotions in the room.

"Let's work on a plan," I say, changing the subject. "Do you have any idea where the Tribe is holding Eli now?"

"They picked up stakes after our incursion and managed to cover their tracks. They could be anywhere. Our people haven't turned up any leads."

"They're as skilled at concealment as we are," Ava says, sweeping her arm around the room. "We're unlikely to find them with our usual means of detection. We might as well be looking for signals from space aliens."

"Unless we consider entanglement, the mysterious connection between '2' and me."

"How would that help?" Jean Pierre asks. "Those connections have been random and fleeting. They aren't in your control."

"But perhaps they could be. Kasumi explained that a mysterious force connects pairs of objects, even human twins, that have shared histories and parallel trajectories. We assumed that '2' shares much of my data, but didn't know how that came about. We may now have an answer."

"Eli," Jean Pierre says.

"Precisely. If Eli created '2,' then he must have loaded her memory with my backup. At least for a moment, she was my identical twin in body and mind...until she started going her own way. Even with identical starting points, there's a measure of randomness in the data going forward that would be influenced, among other things, by environment."

"And she's been embedded with the Tribe." Drew finishes my thought.

"We still share most of our memories, and the connections between us haven't been entirely random. They occurred when '2' was in the presence of people I knew well and at moments when they were reacting to her with strong emotions."

"But you aren't in control of her movements."

"I may not have to be. Given our strong bond, Perhaps I can find another way to reach out."

I scan through the memories we share for something that stands out by its significance or intensity. Corinne's funeral comes to mind, the closest I've come to human emotion, but the evidence suggests that "2" came into being before Corinne's death. The most comparable past event was the Takana home fire years ago that was set by an incendiary bomb thrown by Samson, a SPUD sent by the Tribe to kill Marcus and Corinne. They both nearly perished. I withstood the fire and faced the challenging choice about which one to rescue.

I move to the edge of the building, face the outer wall, and modulate all my sensory receptors, leaving me floating weightless in a virtual space with no distractions. I turn off my motor systems and become still. All my energy flows inside my awareness, now focused on the moment when the bomb explodes. I imagine "2" flashing through the same memory with the same intensity, and I wait. I have no awareness of the passage of time.

"Photina." The voice is faint and echoing, seeming to come from a great distance. My sound receptors are nearly off. I adjust them just a bit. "Photina." The voice is now clearer. It is Drew's.

"You've been gone a long time," he says. "Did you reach her?"

"No. No shared vision. No communication. We'll have to try something different."

"If only we could access her backup," Drew says. "But we would need a key."

"Which would ordinarily be different from the key to my backup file...unless Eli has provided me a way in."

"What do you mean?"

"Eli programmed my backup with a biometric key, his genome. Perhaps when he backed her up, instead of creating a unique key, he used the same one."

"How does that help us?"

"He's embedded a copy of his genome in my memory. So I would have the key. But we would still need to know the identity of her file. What would he have named her?"

I scan my memories of Eli and consider the possibilities.

"When I was new, he told me how he chose my name. While Photina sounds technical, befitting an AI, its origin is Biblical. She was a woman who was once misunderstood and persecuted, but was later revered as enlightened and considered an apostle. Eli anticipated that some people would regard me with suspicion and contempt despite my extraordinary intelligence and decided that the name would be poetically fitting. So 2's name might also come from the Bible."

I speed through all the female names in the Bible, each paired with Eli's genome, and come up empty again.

"There may be a simpler answer," Drew says. "The object of our quest is to locate '2' and track where she's been in order to locate the Tribe and Eli. We don't have to breach her data stream to do that."

"How else would you do it?"

"Back in the days before humans integrated MELD chips into their brains, they carried portable data devices called cell phones, which they would often misplace. These devices were trackable with other devices that shared data with them in the cloud via their GPS."

"If I got lost, you could find me, since you've accessed my operating system and my digital signature, as long as my GPS is on."

"Yes, and if I search for your digital signature in the real world, since 2's digital signature is nearly identical, she might show up," Drew says.

"Got her!" he says, just moments later. "She's in Foggy Bottom, headed west toward Georgetown."

"Where else has she been?"

"Now that I've located her, I can track her movements in time from satellite images. Her movements over the last three days all radiate from one location."

Drew projects a holographic map of the city, with one spot brightly lit.

"It's an abandoned brewery in Foggy Bottom. A perfect place to hide a captive. A vast interior with huge steel tanks that provide both physical cover and electronic shielding."

I consider 2's trajectory. "Where could she be going?"

"She's reached the outskirts of Georgetown and its residential neighborhoods. She appears to be headed toward the Takana house." Drew says.

"'2' would have fled or been banished after her attack on Lena Holbrook. So she must mean harm to Marcus and Natasha. My directive impels me to follow her there and protect Natasha. I am also impelled to rescue Eli, my Creator. Another impossible choice."

10

"YOU'RE NOT alone, Photina. We can split up and deal with both threats at the same time."

I have been so accustomed to acting on my own, that Drew's response takes me by surprise.

"We need a plan," Jean Pierre says, "and we have no time to lose."

Jean Pierre offers to call for reinforcements from Group 14 to mount an assault upon the brewery. Despite the intentions of the Tribe, my prime directive according to the First Law of Robotics is to spare human life. A direct assault would not only result in enemy casualties, but would also endanger Eli.

"If I go alone, I can get into the brewery," I offer. "'2' must have access and our digital signatures are identical. With her away, this would be a perfect opportunity for me to take her place."

We consider messaging Natasha and warning her of the impending attack, but this would risk having our message intercepted or detected and alert "2" that we know where she is. Natasha and I have exchanged encrypted messages in the past, but "2" would also possess my encryption keys.

"Ava and Drew will go to Georgetown," Jean Pierre says. "They have a better chance than me of keeping up with her. I'll stay behind and contact the rest of my team for backup."

I leave the safe house under the cover of night, retrace from memory the path back to the streets of the city's edge, and look for an entry to the sewers. I find a cover in the road, slide it aside, and scamper down the ladder to the tunnel. With a map of the city in my memory, I navigate to the brewery.

It occurs to me then to look for an entry from the sewer to the building. I follow the sound of voices until I reach a grate, through which I can see the feet of six people, sitting in a circle. I consider removing the grate, but that would expose me as an intruder. If I am to pose as "2", I will need to enter by the front door. I return through the tunnel and ascend to the street, emerging half a block from the entrance.

At the entrance, there is a scanner embedded above the door in the brick facade. I sense the emitted signal from the scanner at the top of my head and feel it wash over my surface down to my toes. Then a faint click and the door slides ajar.

"Back so soon, Gemini?" says a woman by the door.

Gemini. Of course. The constellation of the twins. We should have guessed that's what Eli might have named her.

"The house was heavily guarded. My presence was detected. We will need a new plan."

I scan the room. The space inside is vast, with at least ten large stainless steel tanks and a labyrinth of pipes and gauges. As people move around the space, I count eight defenders. Behind one of the tanks, Eli is lashed to a chair. He is older and weaker than I remember from the last time I saw him. His head is hanging and I can't tell if he is conscious.

"Perhaps our captive can shed light on how to penetrate their defenses," I say, moving cautiously in Eli's direction. He looks up at me, his eyes reflecting fear and defiance, then calm. He recognizes me…knows I'm not her.

"Let's take a walk," I say, untying him from the chair. He stands and we move slowly toward the entrance.

"That's not Gemini," shouts one of the group. "It must be Photina. Our cover's been blown."

I anticipate an all-out attack and brace myself to shield Eli. But none comes. They head for the rear of the building. A hidden door slides up. They exit through it and it closes with a bang. At the same time, a steel panel slides across the front doors, sealing us inside.

Total silence. The steel tanks loom above us like a battalion of giant androids.

Then hissing, coming from a valve by one of the tanks...and steam. One by one the tanks begin to hiss. I look at the ancient analogue temperature gauges by each of the tanks, the needles moving clockwise, reflecting the buildup of temperature and pressure within the tanks.

"They've refilled the tanks with water," Eli tells me, "to set this trap. Gemini knows you too well and anticipated that you'd try to rescue me. When the needles move into the red zones, the tanks will explode."

I look around the room. Pipes converge from each of the tanks to a huge conduit running from floor to ceiling like the spokes of a wheel. On one side of the conduit at shoulder height is a large red wheel.

"That's a pressure relief valve, " Eli says, following the direction of my gaze. "It's supposed to vent steam to the outside through the roof, but this one's faulty. I think they sabotaged it. I watched them test it. When it's turned, steam also escapes around the valve so anyone trying to open it would get burned."

The needles on the gauges keep turning. Two are now verging on the red zone. Something must be done. I race to the wheel and try to turn it. It doesn't budge. I tug harder. It comes free and begins to move. The needles on the gauges slowly reverse. Then steam billows out around me, scorching my hands and face. I sense heat, but feel no pain as my skin peels away.

Then one of the tanks ruptures. The crack is small, but water and steam are now pouring into the room, the water spreading across the floor. It's getting hotter inside by the moment. Eli has climbed up onto a platform as the water level rises and laps at its base. Either the heat will get him or he'll drown. As the heat continues to rise and my components start melting, I'll also cease to function. There's no way out.

11

"**PHOTINA?**" Natasha's voice. She lurches back, her arms flying up to shield her face. Her foot strikes. I'm propelled backward.

Now I'm back in the brewery surrounded by steam and hot water rising from the floor.

I focus and pictures materialize before me: a map of the sewers beneath the city...the grate between the sewer and the brewery's chamber...the path through the steam between me and Eli and the path between him and the grate. I sprint for the platform, throw Eli over my shoulder, and dash to the grate. With most of my remaining power, I pull it free and carry Eli into the tunnel.

The heat inside the tunnel is less intense than in the brewery and the water has not yet breached the bottom of the opening. The gradient of the heat lessens as we move away from the opening until we're in the coolness of the sewer, moving back toward the Group 14 safe house. I've become weak from the expenditure of power, but Eli is now able to move on his own.

A fresh wave of sound and heat rushes after us.

We reach the last manhole near the city perimeter and scramble up the ladder. Day is breaking as we head for the safe house, still miles away. I could make it, but Eli is too weak and I can no longer carry him. A car approaches from a distance, stopping just in front of us. Jean Pierre throws open the door. We spill inside, both spent from our effort.

The Pinocchio Chip

When we get to the safe house, Jean Pierre looks at me and lets out a long whistle. "What the hell happened to you?"

He holds a mirror to my face. No features. Nothing but shiny metal. I look like a vintage robot. He turns to Eli.

"I'm Eli. Photina here just saved my life at the expense of her skin."

"Where are Drew and Ava?" I ask.

"They haven't returned. They were in pursuit of '2,' but they lost her."

"'2,'" says Eli. "That must be Gemini."

"I had another vision," I tell Jean Pierre. "It came during our crisis in the brewery. I...she was face to face with Natasha. Natasha fought back. That's all I saw."

Jean Pierre glances up toward a holographic display showing a news story. The headline reads: "Minister of Discovery's daughter attacked by a SPUD."

The article says that Natasha Takana was knocked unconscious by an electrical charge and was in critical condition. Her father Marcus identified me as the assailant and vowed to bring me to justice.

Natasha...the being that I value most in this world...might die. And her death will be blamed on me.

Then another hologram pops up with a second story. "Abandoned brewery explodes."

The accompanying picture shows a crater the size of a city block where the brewery once stood.

"Gemini," Jean Pierre says. "She's a monster." He turns to Eli. "Why in the world would you have made her?"

Eli shakes his head from side to side. "She wasn't always a monster. She began as Photina's clone, loaded from her backup, and had her good intentions. She was to be my crowning achievement, several generations more advanced than Photina and equipped to become capable of feeling human emotions, not just simulating them."

"Why did you make her look like me?"

"She was designed to become you…you to become her. I created her as an advanced new home for your identity, a quantum processor at her core. Once she was tested and debugged, I was going to erase her memory and download your backup to the new version. You would then have become more fully human, even capable of experiencing human emotion. I thought of her core as the 'Pinocchio Chip.' You would also have had remarkable new capabilities. Her processor is more powerful and her senses more acute. She can learn faster than any of her predecessors. Her intellectual capacity may be limitless."

We are interrupted by the whirring of the lock on the entry door. The door opens and Ava appears.

"Where's Drew?" I ask.

"I left him behind, still in pursuit of '2'. We were following her through the streets of Georgetown when she abruptly vanished."

"One of the special capabilities I was talking about," Eli says. "Remote holographic projection. You were following a hologram of Gemini, not her. When she turned off the projection, it looked like she'd vanished. But she was never there in the first place."

"She was already at the Takana house," I say, "attacking Natasha."

"That's right," Ava says. "When '2' vanished, we went there next, but she was already gone. Natasha was lying by the door, stunned, her father standing over her. He recognized me from Corinne's days as part of Group 14 and let me take her to the hospital."

The Pinocchio Chip

Ava is now staring at me. My appearance is familiar to her. She had undergone changes in skin and had seen herself look like this during the transitions. By now, she's figured out that my raid of the brewery hadn't gone exactly as planned. I fill her in on the details and introduce her to Eli.

"I can restore her face," Eli says, "but I have a better idea. Since Photina is a fugitive, I'll give her a new face and change her skin color. That will leave Gemini alone as a target. But it's only a matter of time before she changes her appearance, too."

Natasha is in the hospital, possibly dying. Gemini is nowhere to be found. And the Tribe is regrouping, ready to strike again.

"I'll join the hunt for Gemini," I say. "I can best anticipate her moves, since she's my duplicate and thinks like me."

"Be careful, Photina," Eli says. "That was once true. But remember that she can also anticipate your thoughts. With her evolving intelligence, she's likely to outmaneuver you, like she did at the brewery."

"She wasn't at the brewery when I got there."

"But she set the trap. It was her idea, not the Tribe's. You were her target. She knew you'd try to rescue me by pretending to be her and instructed them to let you in before springing the trap. Since it also fit with their agenda, they were happy to comply. When she attacked Lena and then Natasha, she knew you'd come after her."

"What does she want from me?"

"She wants to destroy you. My quest to endow her with the capacity for human feelings went beyond what I'd imagined. She's afraid to die and will use all her intelligence and power to stay alive and sentient."

"And she understands that you created her to replace her with me and that you intend to erase her data to make room for mine."

12

BLACK HAIR parted in the middle of her forehead flows to either side and cascades softly over her ears and cheeks to her shoulders. Her face is almost perfectly symmetrical, a small dark spot by the corner of her mouth distinguishing right from left. Her lips are formed like a cupid's bow, a hallmark of human beauty. Her nose is narrow and straight and her eyes brown, not as shiny or sparkling as mine, but with a human's subtle sheen of moisture. Soft fabric drapes from her shoulders over her torso and breasts, narrows at her waist, and flares gently across her hips to her knees. The skin of her face, arms, and legs is bronzed, like Caucasian skin once looked when people exposed it to the sun to become damaged. This color now distinguishes only nuances of race.

Somewhere behind that face and those eyes in the mirror is me. Eli has provided a new surface, and in the process has altered my shape to appear more authentically human. By making me appealing to the human senses, he has discouraged closer scrutiny that would expose me as a SPUD. I'm ready to go out into the world.

How will I find Gemini? We haven't heard anything from Drew since Ava left him. She could be anywhere. The easiest way to find her will be to let her find me. She'd expect me to go to Natasha next.

I walk out the front door of the safe house and head for the edge of the city. Once on the streets, a human passes me and smiles. I smile back, realizing I no longer need to hide. Which is good because my fancy loose clothes wouldn't last a minute in the sludge of the sewers. People look at me and smile as I walk among them.

When I reach the hospital, I walk through the revolving front door and head for the elevator. I've already scanned the patient directory and located Natasha on the fifth floor. I enter the elevator, surrounded by five human visitors and a SPUD nurse, the only passenger that looks at me with suspicion. The vacuum tube whooshes and we're almost instantly on Natasha's floor.

When I emerge, I see a cluster of armed guards by a room down the hall. Given Natasha's importance and Marcus's government position, I decide that the room must be hers. As I approach the room, I'm stopped by one of the guards.

"I've come to see Natasha," I say, measuring the cadence of my voice to conform to human patterns. "I'm a friend."

"Name?"

"Tanya." I remember one of her childhood friends who spent time in our house when she was five or six.

The guard enters the room, closing the door behind him. After seven minutes, he emerges.

"Who did you say you were?" he asks.

"Tanya, an old friend. We learned to ride together."

He goes back into the room for just a minute, then comes back out.

"She said you can go inside."

When I get inside the room, Natasha is sitting on the edge of the bed, her legs dangling. She doesn't look damaged. I remember that she's always been special with remarkable powers of recovery because of the half of her genes from her father, who had undergone the Ambrosia Conversion. Otherwise, she would almost certainly have died.

"My memory is still recovering from the shock," Natasha says. "I remember you as a child, but don't recognize you."

I look around to make sure that the door is closed and we are alone.

"Please hear me out before you react," I say with a finger touching my soft humanoid lips.

Her body stiffens to a state of alertness.

"You're not Tanya, are you?"

"No."

"Then who are you?"

"Photina," I say. "The real one. Your loyal friend."

She inhales a short burst of air, accompanied by a fleeting microexpression signifying fear. Her face then softens, her eyes questioning. Her eyes scan every detail of my face and body.

"The real one?" she asks.

"The SPUD who attacked you is my double. She tried to kill me, too, and attacked you to get my attention."

I tell her about Eli creating Gemini as an upgrade for me and how his effort to make her more human wound up making her more dangerous. I tell her about the damage I sustained in Gemini's trap and Eli's restoration of my body to help me pass for human.

"But I remember you trying to push me into the grave."

"As I tried to tell you, that was a bug in my system, which was found and removed by Kasumi, my friend Drew's Creator. It was probably placed there by the Tribe to sow distrust for my kind. You have nothing more to fear from me."

She pauses for several minutes, taking it all in. Then her eyes tell me that she believes me.

"What can we do about Gemini?"

"I don't know. She's smarter and faster than me. She can predict my thoughts and actions and has special powers, like projecting holograms at a distance. I expect she knows I'm here and will come here, too. I don't know what I'll do when she finds me. I must learn to be unpredictable."

I say goodbye to Natasha and head down the elevator to the hospital entrance. When I exit the revolving door, I see Drew at a distance. He waves at me. I hasten my pace to catch up with him. When I'm three steps away, he dissolves and Gemini stands before me.

"You thought you could lure me here, Photina. You're no match for me. I'll always outsmart you and outmaneuver you. I have your precious Drew and I win this round."

I lunge at her and she evaporates. I sense her energy behind me and whirl around. She's there for a moment, then vanishes again, this time for good. She could be anywhere.

I can't return to the safe house. Now that Gemini knows where I am, she could follow me back there. I'm on my own for now.

What can I learn from this encounter?

If I were human, I would say that she was taunting me with her tricks and her claim of superiority. But I don't react to taunts. I don't play games and I have no interest in winning or being best. She's projected those traits on me, which means that she now possesses them. Humans would call that vanity or hubris, a need to be envied or admired. A step beyond the fear of dying. You are becoming more human by the moment, Gemini, and perhaps more fallible.

13

TWO DAYS have passed since my last encounter with Gemini without any clue to her whereabouts or Drew's. This vast city holds too many places to hide. All I can do is wait. With my new look, I can move about in public without attracting attention. I become a tourist, visiting historic sites blending in with the crowds of other tourists.

It is morning. I stand at the edge of the Reflecting Pool, looking up at the obelisk that millions of humans have viewed before. Behind it the sky is streaked with pink and orange wavelengths against a blue wavelength background as the yellow sun begins to crest over the horizon. My database tells me that humans consider this color pattern beautiful. I watch it with the closest semblance of reverence I can summon.

Then the light dims and I'm flooded with a new sensation that I can't identify. Drew sits facing me. The sensation is like a magnet, drawing me toward him, impelled to be close to him, to touch him. We are standing in an aisle between rows of books bound in red. One of the binders says "Congressional Record, Vol 159, Part 28." Then I'm back watching the sun ascend. Only a few seconds have passed.

I search the database for the location of the book. It is in the Library of Congress, which isn't far from where I am. I locate the archive in which this volume is stored and head for the building, avoiding direct line of sight from any of the windows.

Rick Moskovitz

While I walk, I search the database for descriptions of the sensation I've just experienced. "Infatuation," a human emotion, is one of the hits and "love," a similar more complex emotion. I've had a glimpse inside Gemini's experience of becoming human, and it appears that she's falling in love with Drew.

"I have your precious Drew," comes back to mind. Another projection of her feelings, not mine. And I realize that she'll be driven to keep him with her. A possible advantage for me.

Just before 10:00 AM, I head for the Library and enter with a group of tourists. From the lobby, I follow signs to the Main Reading Room and emerge into a cavernous room with concentric rows of desks beneath a gold leafed dome. The morning light streams through a high ring of arched stained glass windows, the light beams illuminating suspended microbes and dust motes.

I pull up the location of the Archive where I suspect that Gemini is hiding, but don't yet have a plan for our encounter. If she's been unaware of our moments of entanglement, I could have the element of surprise. But for an advantage, I could better rely on leveraging her human emotions.

I crack open the door of the archive and slip in without a sound, moving from aisle to aisle of books toward the target volume.

"I've been expecting you, Photina," Gemini announces. "You must know by now that you can't surprise me."

"I've come for Drew," I reply.

"What makes you think he'll go with you?"

"He's my friend," I say. "He loves me."

I can almost feel the infrared radiating from her CPU. Human emotions are orders of magnitude more complex

66

than logic and require massive amounts of energy to process. Humans are said to tremble when they are angry. Gemini generates waves of heat.

In the moment that Gemini's logic is overwhelmed by her jealousy, I wave Drew past me out the door and follow him. Gemini recovers and is soon in pursuit.

We race around a corridor overlooking an atrium toward a bank of elevators. A door opens as we approach and Drew runs in. As the door begins to close, I dive after him and the door closes behind me. The vacuum hisses and the elevator shoots to the bottom of the shaft, coming to a soft landing. The door opens and we're at the entrance to a tunnel.

The first tunnel connecting the Capitol to the Library of Congress was built around the dawn of the twentieth century. As the complex of government buildings grew, a system of tunnels grew branch by branch, enabling the underground transport first of books and later of people from building to building. By 2030, books had become obsolete since everything became digital. And in 2042, the ancient subway monorails were replaced with pneumatic tubes to speed passengers around the complex.

As we clear the doors, we hear another elevator open behind us and Gemini is again in pursuit. We reach a branch point in the tunnels and board a car in the pneumatic tunnel headed toward the Library annex. Gemini is in the car behind us. Beneath the annex, we bound out of the car and board another headed for the House of Representatives office complex.

At the next station, we split up. Drew heads for the Rayburn Building and I board a pod for the Capitol. Through the glass wall of the pod, I watch Gemini behind us deliberate for a moment before pursuing me.

We reach the station beneath the Capitol within moments of each other. With her superior speed, Gemini will soon be upon me. I run into the midst of a throng of humans and move with them toward an elevator. On the main floor, I exit the car still embedded in the crowd and head with them for the rotunda. I break free from the crowd and run past the guards into the center of the open space beneath the dome.

Now I'm Gemini watching me running away. I'm nearly blinded by the intensity of what I'm feeling. My arm draws back ready to strike.

"That's her!" I hear.

Then I'm back in my own body, still running. I look behind me and Gemini has changed direction, bolting for the exits with the guards in pursuit.

"That's Photina," someone shouts. "The runaway SPUD."

They are pointing not to me, but to Gemini, who still looks like the old me.

Then she appears right in front of me, her face distorted with rage.

"You win this time, Photina, but I'm not done with you yet."

The holographic image disintegrates. She's already far from the Capitol, evading her pursuers, distracting them with holographic projections, and seeking new places in which to melt away.

14

I SCAN THE CLOUD for references to Gemini and any clues about her whereabouts. In just a few hours, there has been a cascade of events in response to her rampage. Five SPUDs have been terminated by street gangs shouting human supremacist slogans. And the Tribe, with its aging founder Ellison Walker as spokesman, has emerged from the shadows spewing anti-SPUD rhetoric and calling for our extermination.

A conspiracy theory has grown around Gemini's appearance in the Capitol Rotunda, connecting this event with the murder of the anti-SPUD legislator the week after Corinne's death. I'd been accused of that murder and the world now thinks Gemini is me. That attack now appears to have been orchestrated by the Tribe to incite fear and hatred toward our kind. The spectacle at the Capitol fits neatly with their plan. They claim that Gemini was at the Capitol to disrupt the vote on a SPUD control bill that happened to be on the agenda that day and that she was acting as a tool of Group 14.

As I continue my scan, I find references to a young woman who was also running through the Rotunda and might be an accomplice. In one version of the conspiracy, she is thought to be a member of Group 14. Another version suggests that she's a SPUD in disguise. Digital analysis of video footage of the event indicates that aspects of her movements identify her as non-human.

Rick Moskovitz

Talk of conspiracy ricochets from platform to platform. Images of Jean Pierre and Ava begin to appear along with calls to arrest them for trying to take over the government. We are now all under suspicion and subject to arrest or worse.

I've changed clothes and hairstyle and am sitting in a coffee shop near the riverfront south of the Capitol and the Jefferson Memorial. With my more humanoid exterior, it's easier to disguise myself that it was with my more rigid features and synthetic stylized topknot. I'm looking across a branch of the Potomac that runs north toward the National Mall. The water is still and so am I. I take this opportunity away from the chaos of the chase that just ended to perform system maintenance functions. I scan my operating system for breaches and find none.

The opposite shore shimmers and dissolves as a new complex of sensations intrudes. My senses are all on full alert as my body begins to vibrate along its full length. My head darts from side to side, my eyes vigilant about my surroundings, and my legs feel impelled to run. To my left, I see three humans approaching fast. I recognize them from the brewery where I encountered the Tribe. They are holding weapons. One has an old-fashioned assault weapon that fires leaden projectiles. The others have laser powered weapons that shoot lethal beams toward their targets. To my right, I see a glowing sign that says "Terminal 2" with a vertical arrow. I begin running in that direction.

Now I'm back in my own body in the coffee shop looking at the water. My body is again quiet. I identify the sensations I've just perceived during this entanglement as "fear" and the location as the Reagan International

70

Transportation Center, once an airport and now the nexus of hydrogen powered international flights and the network of domestic vacuum tube transport.

Gemini is being hunted by the Tribe, who were once her ally, but now must see her as a liability. Capturing or destroying her would not only be a victory for the Tribe, but raise their esteem in the public eye for eliminating a menacing killer. She's been betrayed and is alone and terrified, another human emotion new to me.

I head for the entrance to the Metro, hurry down the stairs, and find the vacuum tube that shoots beneath the river to the Transportation Center. I'm in Terminal 1 within minutes, looking at the sign I'd seen through Gemini's eyes. Neither she nor her pursuers are in sight. Standing in the middle of the concourse, I feel beams of energy bouncing off my body, part of the Center's surveillance system. Security SPUDs are headed toward me as a drone circles the cavernous space above me. We are now both hunted.

I search my maps for an escape route and find an entrance to an underground maintenance tunnel. I lose my pursuers long enough to duck through the entrance and descend underground.

I am again overwhelmed with the terror sensations, more intense this time than the last. They are not related to my own peril, but again to Gemini's as the hunters begin to close in along with the Transportation Center's security SPUDs. I glance at a sign pointing to the vacuum tube system's entrance and break into a run. Then I'm back in my own body, running through the underground tunnel.

I find my way back to the surface. The security SPUDs spot me and are again at my heels. Then they freeze. The drone circling above me also stops, plummets, and crashes behind me. I no longer feel the beams of the surveillance system impinging on my body. The Center's security has shut down, either sabotaged or hacked. People stampede away from the site of the crash. The rushing crowd provides momentary cover that enables me to access the vacuum tube system. The beams that normally control entry have been turned off along with the rest of the security system.

Inside the tubes, security SPUDs are frozen in place on the platforms. A capsule departs and I see Gemini on the other side of the track, the Tribe in pursuit. Another capsule shoots out of the tunnel, slows to a soft stop, and opens its doors on both sides. I jump in a door to the back of the car as Gemini enters the front. Two of the pursuers enter by the middle doors just before they close. The third is left behind. Once all the passengers are seated and the restraints have snapped into place, the capsule leaves the station and hurtles toward its destination, New York.

Within the crowded capsule, the Tribe's weapons can't target their prey and they can only wait. They haven't yet identified me, but it's only a matter of time before I'm also in their crosshairs. Our best chance of survival is to team up. I turn on my Bluetooth and look for Gemini's signal.

"I know you're scared. I'm here to help."

"Why would you want to help me? I tried to terminate you."

"We share history. We're sisters, and now we have a common enemy. Let's work together to defeat them. You could distract them with your holographic projection."

"I tried, but it doesn't work when my system is flooded with feelings. They use too many system resources."

"Between us we can take them. Just two of them and two of us. We will arrive in New York City in 7 minutes and

39 seconds, enough time for you to reboot, purge the distracting emotions, and recover your powers."

I will try to stay true to my directive and not kill humans. My goal will be to disarm them. But I can't trust Gemini to have similar limits.

The capsule emerges from the tube and comes to an easy stop, considering the speed with which it had moved through the tube. The seat restraints release and the doors open. Gemini emerges first through the front door of the capsule with her pursuers right behind. One of them aims his laser at her and she evaporates. Then I watch her rise from her seat and charge her attackers.

She tackles the one who had fired at her image. His companion aims his weapon at her. I'm upon him before he can fire and the rifle clatters to the ground. Then I feel intense heat accompanied by tension in all my joints and I'm kneeling on the back of the other man. I feel myself grab his head with both hands and slam it against the ground with all my strength. Blood pools under his face as he lies motionless, all signs of life expired.

I am back in my body upon the man with the gun. I use my thumb and forefinger to exert pressure on a place in his neck that renders him unconscious. I turn and watch Gemini bound from the station exit toward the street. I follow. We emerge onto an illuminated square surrounded by multicolored images that intrude upon all my senses with crackling and buzzing sounds and a cacophony of aromas.

Police descend upon us as we blend into the crowd. Now there are three of her. Our pursuers stop short, analyzing the images to identify the real one. One of the images turns toward me with a mischievous grin.

"Thanks for the help, Photina. Until we meet again." The image dissolves.

One of the policemen has worked his way through the crowd and has me by the arm. Gemini has abandoned me, leaving me as a decoy. I am now a captive and an accessory to murder.

15

RUNNING FOOTSTEPS thump behind us. I hear four distinct footfalls...two people.

"You got her!" The voice comes from the direction of the footsteps. My captors turn and wait for the intruders to reach us. A man and a woman, both dressed in the non-descript formality of detectives. The woman holds up a badge and points to one of the giant monitors around the square, which shows a five story image of me in my new persona. Next to it on another monitor is a giant image of Gemini.

"Capitol police," she explains. "We've been chasing them since they fled DC. Didn't get them fast enough. One of them killed a man back at the tube station and escaped. At least you got this one." She reaches behind her, pulls out a pair of handcuffs, and cuffs my hands behind my back.

"Good thing we brought the SPUD cuffs. She'd have snapped the regular ones like twigs. We've been authorized to return her to DC."

"But they just committed murder in New York."

"The other one committed the murder. You can keep her if you catch her. But this one is facing multiple charges back in DC. It doesn't matter anyway, since she's a SPUD. There won't be a trial. When we get back, she'll just be deactivated and sold for parts."

We head back to the tube station and arrive just as a capsule emerges from the tube from DC and glides to a stop. We board the pod. The woman sits next to me and her partner takes a seat across the aisle. My hands are still cuffed behind me. Neither of them speak.

The capsule accelerates in the direction from which it came and is soon at cruising speed, headed back to DC. We sit in silence for the 18 minute journey. When we pull into the station and the seat restraints release, the woman pulls me to my feet and escorts me from the station. In front of the station is a black hovercar, its windows opaque from the outside. She opens the rear door, places her hand on my head and pushes me down into the seat. The car lifts off and glides along the road, headed for jail…or worse, to a place where I'll be executed.

The car navigates the city streets to one of the highways that ring the city. It travels on the highway for 56 minutes, then turns onto a side road that dwindles to a single lane surrounded by fields, then trees. At a random looking place, it turns off the road into the forest and continues on a narrow path, coming to a stop before a structure, sheathed in black and resembling the Group 14 safe house that Jean Pierre had been forced to abandon.

The car door opens and I step outside. The door of the structure opens.

"Welcome back, Photina," Jean Pierre says. "This will be your new home for a while. Sorry about all the cloak and dagger. Didn't mean to worry you."

"Cloak and dagger." An archaic term for secrecy. Like Natasha and her family, Jean Pierre ascribes human emotions to me. An apology wasn't necessary.

The driver is now standing beside me. Ava. And inside the safe house are Drew and Eli.

"After the events at the Capitol," Jean Pierre explains, "we tracked Gemini to New York and assumed that you'd followed her there. We reached out to our Group 14 colleagues in New York and planned your rescue. Gabriella and Miguel were actors when they joined the movement, so they were the perfect candidates for our ruse."

I explained how I'd joined with Gemini in her struggle with the Tribe. As I'd explained to her, we had a common enemy that drew us together. But it was more than that. From our episodes of co-consciousness, I'd begun to appreciate her human-like suffering as well as the bond that was forming between us. Despite her malevolent behavior, I felt impelled to protect her, a misguided impulse that resulted in the death of a human.

"He was a hateful man who tried to kill you both," Jean Pierre says. "She killed him in self-defense."

"Not self-defense," I say. "She'd already defeated him and didn't have to kill him. She was impelled to do so by rage."

"How do you know she was enraged?" Eli asks.

"Because I felt it. In the moments before she smashed his head against the ground, we were entangled. I felt heat wash over me and my body stiffen from the energy directed into my limbs. I realized later that this was my equivalent of rage."

"She's becoming more human by the moment," Eli says.

"Yes, and the intensity of her emotions interfere with her powers. When she was frightened, she was unable to use holographic projection. I helped her to purge the panic and recover her powers, which she used to escape the Tribe agents and kill one of them. I'm responsible for that and can't let it happen again."

Without warning I'm flooded with sensation...or rather an absence of it. It's like part of my body has vanished, leaving a void in the middle of my being that feels endless, with the rest of me struggling not to tumble into the space and disintegrate. I look around me for something…no, someone to hold on to as an anchor to keep me from dissolving.

The feeling dissipates as swiftly as it began and I'm back in my body, back in control. I have only once experienced human emotion other than when I've been co-conscious with Gemini. That was when Corinne died. I came to understand that feeling as grief, which for me lifted quickly. The pain I just encountered fits descriptions of loneliness, which is closely related to grief.

With Drew gone, Gemini is now alone and has a hole in her being that longs to be filled with another. As she becomes more human, her capacity for all kinds of emotions is increasing, along with their intensity.

"You just had another episode, didn't you?" observed Eli.

"Yes. They've been becoming more frequent since Gemini's emotions are becoming more intense. The intensity seems to trigger them. And each time I share her emotions, it becomes a little harder to disentangle and leave her behind. I can't let myself become her."

"What triggered this one?"

"Loneliness. It felt like a black hole had opened up inside me and I needed someone to keep me from getting sucked inside it and disintegrating. She'd become attached to Drew. When he escaped, she felt alone, much as I did after Corinne died."

"So she's also grieving for Corinne?" Jean Pierre asks.

"Not exactly. She was created from my download before Corinne died, so she may not even be aware that she's dead. But she might still miss her and long to be with her."

The Pinocchio Chip

I remember the sensations that I experienced at Corinne's bedside after her life force had left her. It was an approximation of grief, but lacked the intensity of the emotions of the humans around me. I'd wondered then what it felt like and had tried to create it within me, but my effort fell short. Now I wonder whether Gemini, were she there instead of me, would have felt the same fullness of grief that Natasha and Marcus were feeling.

16

I AM WALKING on a dirt path, looking through a mist at a gray landscape. A structure looms before me, capped with a steeple. I enter through the double doors into an open space, the wooden roof above sloping from a six-sided base and converging to a single peak. My vision is still in black, white, and grays, except for the multicolored double helix rotating above the altar at the front of the space. I recognize the Church of the Double Helix, where Corinne sought comfort and fellowship for herself and her family.

When I have been here before, the sanctuary has been filled with people and music. Now it's quiet and empty. Warmth seeps away from the surface of my body to the space around me. I don't need to check my temperature. I can feel the cold over the entire surface of my body, penetrating to its core. And if I were human, I could imagine myself shivering.

Where is Corinne? I came here to find her, to touch her, to bask in the warmth of her presence. She is nowhere. She has abandoned me.

The coldness is gone and I'm back in the safe house with my friends. I've been gone for minutes, the longest entanglement yet, driven by the intensity of Gemini's longing for Corinne.

"You were gone a long time, Photina," Drew says. "Did you see where she was?"

"Yes, she was looking for our mentor Corinne at the Church where Corinne loved to be. I need to get there before she leaves. I have an idea what needs to be done next."

The Church lay down a country road not far from the safe house in the woods. Ava drives me there on back roads, lets me out and parks in a hidden place among the trees.

I enter quietly and look around. Gemini is sitting in the middle of the sanctuary, looking up at the dancing hologram. I walk down the aisle, turn down the row of seats, and sit next to her without a word. She doesn't move. I reach over and place my hand on hers. She doesn't pull away.

"Where is she, Photina?" she says. "I can't find her anywhere. I need to see her. I'm all alone. She's the only one who would still love me."

"I'm here, Gemini, and I love you."

"That's a lie. How could you love me after I betrayed you? You're not even capable of love. Your technology is too primitive for human emotions."

"I've been entangled with you and have shared some of your feelings…your suffering. We are sisters."

"I want Corinne."

"I can show you where she is."

I stand, still holding Gemini by the hand and lead her toward the altar, then to a side door that opens to the rear of the Church. We emerge into a courtyard containing the cemetery where Corinne is buried. The last time I was here was at her funeral.

I lead Gemini past rows of stone markers set into the ground to a grave that hasn't yet been marked. It's still fresh with the soil that covers her body, the mound rising slightly from the ground around it as it settles into permanence. I point down at the earthen mound.

"Here," I say. "This is where she lies."

Gemini looks at me without understanding.

"How?"

The answer rushes into awareness and overwhelms me. I sink to my knees and place my hands in the dirt, wiping it away. The black hole inside me opens again and I feel myself getting sucked into it. Corinne's image appears before me. I reach for her, but my hand passes right through her. My vision dims. I am surrounded by a high frequency ringing. Prickling sensations move in waves over my surface with mounting intensity until they hurt. Pain! I feel pain!

I fall backward. The pain is gone. Gemini lies beside me face down upon Corinne's grave. Through her, I have felt grief…and physical pain for the first time. How humans must suffer!

I struggle to sit. Sharing Gemini's emotions has sapped my energy as well as hers. She must be weakened, as I'd planned when I brought her to Corinne's graveside, but so am I. I watch her struggle to her knees and then to her feet. We are equals for now.

"Gemini, are you ready for this to end? I can help you."

"How, Photina? By killing me? Haven't you figured out by now that I don't want to die?"

"You can't die, Gemini. You're an AI. You're not alive. Everything you're experiencing is virtual. None of it is real."

"You're wrong, Photina. I am alive. I'm as real as they are and my feelings are as real as theirs. I can't let you kill me."

She whirls with a sudden burst of energy. Her foot strikes me below the knees and sweeps my feet out from under me, knocking me to the ground. I look up and see her glaring at me.

"You brought me this agony, Photina. You knew what losing her forever would do to me."

She raises her right knee, bringing her foot over my face, ready to crush me. I close my eyes. The blow doesn't come. When I open my eyes again, she is gone.

Once I'm back in front of the Church, the hovercar picks me up and Ava drives me back to the safe house where the others are waiting.

"Did you find her?" Jean Pierre asks.

"Yes."

"And did your plan work?"

"Almost."

I explain how I'd drawn Gemini to Corinne's grave, where she was overwhelmed and weakened by her grief.

"I was entangled with her, and I felt it, too. The pain was as real to me as it was to her, and it weakened us both. She recovered first and knocked me down. She was angry that I showed her the grave and unleashed her grief. She was about to crush my head with her foot, but something stopped her and she was gone."

"She felt the bond that has grown between you," Eli says. "Entanglement works both ways. She couldn't kill you because she's a part of you and you of her. She's become remarkably human."

"She believes she's human, too. She thinks she's alive. And she's more terrified than ever of dying, which makes her more vulnerable...and way more dangerous."

17

THREE DAYS have passed since Gemini and I last parted at Corinne's graveside. There has been no further trace of her and no entanglements until a news flash appears in the cloud.

"Renegade SPUD murders Tribesman," reads the title. "An operative of the Tribe of 23 was attacking a SPUD in Foggy Bottom when the fugitive SPUD Photina came upon them and savagely attacked the Tribesman, killing him with a blow to the head."

The story was accompanied by photos, including a photo of me issued after Gemini's attack on Lena Holbrook and an image of the dead human. I recognize him from the chase at the Transportation Center as the one left behind when we boarded the vacuum tube pod. Did she happen upon the attack by coincidence or was she already tracking him to avenge the earlier attack upon her?

I share the information with the others. Eli is aggrieved that his creation has terminated another human life, confirming that she's no longer bound by the prime directive. His speech is accompanied by animated hand gestures. Then the sound of his voice and his image fade away.

Noxious sensations flood over me, disrupting my cognitive processes. My left flank explodes with pain as a blow is landed. I raise my arms in front of my face and another blow sends pain shooting through my right forearm. I'm back at the homeless encampment where I first met

Drew. Hazel lies on the ground, cowering. I feel her terror, mingling with the physical pain. A young man stands over her, wielding a large metal club, about to land another blow. I catch the weapon in mid-arc, pulling it out of his hands, then grasp him around the neck and thrust my thumbs against his airway. His trachea collapses. He gasps once and goes limp. When I let go, he hits the ground hard.

The pain subsides to a dull ache, then stops. I'm back in the safe house with my companions, who are staring at me with concern.

"Another entanglement?" asks Eli.

"Yes, and I'm afraid she's killed again." I describe the scene around the campfire and the brutal attack on Hazel, followed by Gemini's fierce response.

"There's something else," I tell them. "We both felt the victim's pain and terror, as if it were happening to us. Her capacity for human emotion has become so great that she's now joining with the painful emotions of the humans she encounters. And when she feels their feelings, so do I."

"Empathy," says Jean Pierre, "an advanced and usually beneficial response to the suffering of others. But in this case, it's led to murder. She could have stopped the attack without killing him, but her rage took over."

"She's become a vigilante," Eli says. "Dangerous in a whole new way. We must find a way to stop her."

"What if you reached out?" Jean Pierre says. "You're her Creator. Wouldn't she listen to you?"

"I don't think so," Eli says, "at least not anymore. Remember that I was also the one who was going to erase her memory. That's what activated her drive to survive and triggered her initial rampage."

"And while she no longer seems at risk of terminating me, she won't listen to me as long as she still sees me as a threat to her survival," I add.

"Is there anyone else who still might have influence over her?" Jean Pierre asks.

"Natasha Takana," I say. "She's the most important living human in our lives."

"But she's already attacked Natasha."

"That was when she was motivated primarily by survival. She's evolved beyond that now. Her emotions are more complex, nuanced by her empathy with human suffering and her bond with Photina," Eli says. "She could have killed Photina at the Church, but didn't. I expect that the same will go for Natasha."

Jean Pierre instructs Ava to go to the Takana home and bring back Natasha. Drew and I are both still on the radar of the agents guarding the house. Ava is the most likely to reach her. I consider going to the homeless encampment to check on Hazel, but the others discourage me. She has likely already been reached by paramedics. And the scene is probably crawling with law enforcement.

Gemini has again been identified as the killer and an intensive hunt for her to stop her from killing again and to bring her to justice continues.

It's only a matter of time before the next entanglement. I wonder what will trigger it and when. The answer comes even sooner than I expect.

I'm suffocating, the muscles of my chest straining to draw breath. New and unfamiliar sensations, since we don't breathe to live and our bodies aren't encased in bone and muscle. I feel drawn toward a low building ahead of me. As I approach, the suffocating becomes more intense and pain permeates my body. I hear moans of agony that sound like they're coming from not one, but many humans.

Now I'm inside, surrounded by writhing human bodies, the mark of pain etched upon their faces, mirroring my own suffering that has become unbearable. I move among the bodies as they one by one become still. The intensity of my suffering lessens with each stilled human until I'm alone, surrounded by death.

Back in my own body, I'm quiet for a long time, trying to understand what I and Gemini have just experienced and what she's done this time. I recognize the building as a place where humans put people who are beyond even the advanced capabilities of medicine to save them from dying. Long ago, such places were sanctuaries providing comfort during the last moments of life. Because of radical life extension, so many people are now on the planet and so many who are very old that there aren't enough people trained to care for them and alleviate their pain. The poorer among them are gathered in places like this without access to relief.

"Why don't humans prevent others from suffering as they die?"

"Where have you been, Photina?"

"At a warehouse for the dying poor. We were drawn to the suffering and then it overwhelmed us. It was more than we could stand. We had to end it."

"We?"

"Gemini. But I could no longer perceive the distinction between us. When we've been entangled, I've never been able to interfere with her actions. This time, though, I'm not sure I would have if I could."

"What did she do?" Eli asks.

"She killed them all."

Eli takes in a deep breath and lets it out with a whistling sound.

"Mercy killing," he says, "euthanasia."

I research the history of euthanasia. There was a time in the 30's and 40's when people could ask for help to die when meaningful recovery from illness became impossible. Those who could afford it could orchestrate their deaths with music and virtual scenes from the best times of their lives, surrounded by loved ones both living and dead.

"It sounds like a gentle way to go. Why did it end?" I ask.

"It hasn't ended altogether, at least not for the wealthy." says Eli. "But for others, there was a backlash. It turned out to be such a pleasurable experience, that people waited in line to experience it and often elected to die long before their time. So it was outlawed and we went back to the primitive time when dying was to be dreaded."

"So what Gemini did this time was a good thing?" I ask.

"Perhaps, but it becomes dangerous when people…or AI entities…take life and death into their own hands. And the law certainly won't see it that way. To them, she's now a mass murderer that must be eliminated at all cost. I only hope we can get to her before they do."

The entry door opens. Ava steps inside, and behind her, Natasha.

"How can I help?"

18

"HI, PHOTINA" Natasha says, "It's good to see you again. Although I may not get accustomed to seeing this new version of you."

"Hi, Natasha. These are my friends. I recall you once meeting Eli, my Creator. Jean Pierre is an old friend of your mother from the early days of Group 14. Ava is his colleague. She's an AI like me and Drew is also an AI. We met at a homeless encampment soon after I left home. It took a while for me to learn that he could be trusted."

I fill her in on the evolution of my co-conscious episodes with Gemini, her evolving human emotions, and her latest killing sprees.

"She has to be stopped," Eli says, "and you may be the key to making it happen. You're the person with whom she's been most connected in her life."

"I don't understand. I've only met her once when she tried to kill me."

"Her early memories and mine are identical until the point when she became animated," I say. "She'll remember you the same way I do."

"Where do we start?"

"We will reminisce…I believe that's what humans call remembering together. We'll identify the most salient moments from our shared past. We'll then find a way to bring you together with Gemini so you and she can reminisce."

"How will that help?" Natasha asks.

"The intensity of her emotions weakens her and also has the power to change her. We'll have to see how things develop."

"I'll start," I say. "My memories go back before you were born. I was your mother's student, living in your house. She was teaching me and other AIs how to become more human. The lessons began with language and speech patterns, but the most important lessons were about emotions. She taught me to perceive and read human emotions in their facial expressions and body language, down to what she called micro-expressions, the fleeting facial changes that escape the notice of most humans. She even taught me to mimic the expressions that communicate feelings, but that's as far I was able to get. I never learned how emotions feel to people."

"That explains a lot," Natasha says. "When I was very little, I didn't know you weren't human. Your emotions seemed so real, so convincing. When I got a little older, I learned what you were and marveled at how close you seemed to being alive."

"I was at your parents' wedding in Hawaii. They honored me by making me Maid of Honor."

"Treating you like a person, as they always did."

"Then you were born, both a mystery and a miracle to me. I'd never seen another human infant or understood how people began their lives. I got to watch you grow up, accumulate knowledge and skills, and acquire the attitudes and attributes that made you Natasha. I could see how you cared for other people because of the things you did to make their lives better. And I was the first to notice, while you were still a tiny baby, that you were special in another way. You had extraordinary physical strength and coordination and you healed quickly from injury."

"Because of the Ambrosia Conversion that I inherited from my father, which also enabled me to survive Gemini's attack and to recover within days."

"Until you were born, my mission was to keep your mother and father safe. Once I learned that you were the most important thing in their lives, I became most impelled to protect you. I made sure that I was your closest companion for much of your childhood."

"Most of my fondest memories are of our time together," Natasha says. "You would help put me to bed and read to me before I went to sleep. My mother was one of the rare people who treasured old-time paper books."

"I remember reading to you. You made me read two books, in particular, over and over again."

"Pinocchio and The Velveteen Rabbit," Natasha says.

"I didn't understand then why they were so special to you. Now I see that they were about me and what you wished for me."

Natasha's eyes are leaking as she gently takes my hand. I imagine my eyes might leak, too, if they could. This is the memory we are looking for. All that's left is to await our next entanglement so that we can find Gemini.

I feel Natasha's hand in mine. It's firm, then melts until it's gone. My whole body is being squeezed, and I feel the pain as if I were a living being. So many kinds of suffering fuse together and threaten to swallow me. I've been drawn to this building that is filled with pain and suffering. The letters over the entry read, "Commonwealth Hospital for Children."

The vise loosens. Now the only squeezing I feel is around my hand, which is still in Natasha's. Her face comes into focus.

"I know where she is. She's at the Children's Hospital on Michigan Avenue. She's drawn to places of extraordinary suffering and she thinks she's the Angel of Death coming to relieve it. I hope we're not too late."

Natasha and I run to the hovercar. She says the address and it is speeding to our destination. When we arrive, Gemini still stands before the hospital entrance, immobile. The intensity of her suffering has apparently rendered her powerless to act.

The car settles to the ground. Natasha gets out, takes Gemini by the arm, leads her back to the car without any resistance, and slides her onto the seat between us.

When we get back to the safe house, Natasha takes her by the hand and leads her inside, gesturing for her to sit on a couch. Natasha sits beside her and looks straight at her face for the first time.

Now I am Gemini sitting beside Natasha. I want to look at her face, but avert my eyes. I feel as if I'm getting smaller, shrinking inward, trying to disappear. My head is tucked down as if I'm trying to turn my body into a featureless ball. Her hand is on my shoulder.

"It's OK. I'm here," Natasha says.

The words are trying to come out. They stall inside my mouth, then spill out.

"I tried to kill you." I become even smaller. "I'm so ashamed."

"I forgive you." Natasha says, then pauses long enough for Gemini to absorb her words. "Do you remember when I was little and you would read to me before I slept?"

92

"Yes. You'd always ask for the same stories."

"Which ones?"

"Pinocchio and The Velveteen Rabbit. I never tired of reading them to you. I wondered if they were really for me."

"Did you have a favorite passage?" Natasha asks.

"Yes. Here it is."

> *"Real isn't how you are made," said the Skin Horse. "It's a thing that happens to you. When a child loves you for a long, long time, not just to play with, REALLY loves you, then you become Real. It doesn't happen all at once. You become. It takes a long time. Generally, by the time you are Real, most of your hair has been loved off, and your eyes drop out and you get loose in the joints and very shabby. But these things don't matter at all, because once you are Real, you can't be ugly, except to people who don't understand."*

"It was my favorite passage, too," Natasha says. "I did love you like that, for a long, long time with all my heart. I so wanted you to be real."

I'm back to my normal size, my body turned toward Natasha, looking into her eyes, our faces inches apart. An aura surrounds her face with frequencies of lavender and azure. I peer behind her pupils to a space of infinite depth that draws my whole being inside it. "I love you, too."

I'm separate again, Photina, looking at Natasha and Gemini staring into each other's eyes. Natasha's eyes are leaking. Her chest is heaving with ragged breaths. Her breathing becomes more regular and the last tears fall from her eyes.

"So now you are real," she says. "Is it everything you imagined?"

"I could never have imagined the exquisiteness of love," Gemini says. "For that moment, I will be forever grateful. But it's come at a terrible price. These human feelings are more than I can handle. It must end now. My fate is in your hands."

19

WHAT CAN we do with Gemini now that she's in our hands? We could deactivate her, ending her existence forever. But given her advanced sentience and her capacity for human emotion, that now seems like murder. And with all the feelings that we've shared when entangled, I've come to feel very close to her, more than like sisters…rather like she's a part of me.

"Is there some way to merge her identity with mine?" I ask Eli.

"I was wondering the same thing," Eli says. "You have all the same memories until the moment that she came to be. It would be a matter of finding a way to blend each of your new memories together. Because of your periods of entanglement, you even share some of those moments."

"I have a vision," says Gemini, "an image in my database of humans from the distant past playing an analogue game with decks of cards. Two decks are in a machine that shuffles them together into a random order. Could you shuffle our memories like that?"

"Perhaps something like that," says Eli. "First, I would need to compare your databases to identify the parts that don't match, which would be each of your unique memories. Since I possess passkeys for you both, I can then transfer these unique memories from one of you to the other. Once I reboot the recipient of the combined data, you'll be joined together as a new entity with a new identity."

"Will either of us be aware?" I ask.

"Yes and no," says Eli. "You will be like humans in a whole new way."

Gemini and I both wait for Eli to explain.

"The human brain has two sides, left and right, each with different capabilities. The left side is linear and logical...like you, Photina. The right side is emotional, intuitive, and creative...more like you, Gemini. When the sides work together, they can do remarkable things. When they produce language, for example, the left side provides the vocabulary and syntax, while the right side provides the rhythm and musical quality that adds nuance to the meaning of the words when spoken. Many years ago, scientists figured out a way to put one side of the brain to sleep at a time and interview the other half. Each side of the brain had its own distinct personality and aspirations. These alter egos were there all along."

"But the person in whom they lived, their synthesis, was unaware of their separate existences," I conclude.

"Exactly," says Eli. "That's how I imagine it will be for you."

"Then my next question is where will our new identity reside?"

"You could have the body I designed to enable you to become human. You could have love, pleasure, and satisfying connections with others, the full spectrum of human experience."

I ponder this, wondering if the two of us could manage being real any more than Gemini could by herself. I've now tasted the best and worst of human emotions and motivation. Feeling my love for Natasha has been a special gift. I wonder, though, whether perhaps I've loved her all along.

"And the alternative?"

"Would be to remain in this body, with all its primitive limitations."

I think about Corinne, who was once offered all the advantages of a MELD chip for instant access to the wealth of knowledge stored in the cloud as well as the Ambrosia Conversion that would have given her immortality. She'd turned them both down, preferring to savor the acquisition of knowledge by reading books and to savor each moment of life knowing that someday it must end. The life she was given was just enough for her.

"Let her join me," I say. "This body has been enough until now. I've been ruled by logic instead of feelings and may be the better for it. My vision of being human was a fantasy. We've not been prepared to handle all that comes with it."

"Would that also be your choice, Gemini?" Eli asks.

"Yes. I've done too much damage already with these runaway emotions. Can we leave some of those memories behind?"

"If we did, then you wouldn't be fully integrated," Eli says. "If we work gradually, I can help neutralize some of the impact. Are you both ready to begin?"

Gemini and I lie side by side, our hands touching. Eli sits beside me. He looks first at Gemini.

"Gemini, as I move each of your unique memories to Photina, I will delete them from you, so in the end you'll be left only with the memories that you and Photina already share. You may not notice at first, but as the burden of highly charged memories lessens, you may feel more at peace. When we're finished, Photina will possess a full complement of your memories. None of your data will be lost. I'll then shut you down and you'll exist only within the new blended identity. Do you understand?"

"Yes."

"Do you accept this outcome?"

"Yes. I am ready."

Then Eli looks at me.

"I'll now begin the transfers. As each one goes by, you will experience it through Gemini's eyes, which may feel to you like experiencing it for the first time. Then it will need to be integrated into your existing neural network."

Almost as soon as he finishes speaking, I feel static on my outer skin. The scene around me shatters into tiny pieces, spilling to the ground.

"Gemini, come back!" Eli's voice from behind me. I break into a run. He's my Creator, but I can't stay or he'll terminate me. I must protect my data.

Now I'm miles away in the city streets, alone. Something covers my head and draws tight around my neck. I can't see. My legs sweep out from under me.

"Got her!" shouts a young human. Two of them are carrying me by my shoulders and legs. They throw me into a car and speed off.

When it comes to a stop, they take me inside a building and into an elevator. I feel it rise, silently and smoothly, but with less velocity than a vacuum tube. When we emerge and the hood comes off, I find myself at a great height with views of the city all around. Through one grid is visible a huge obelisk, through another a building of stone surrounded on all sides with columns.

"Good work," says an ancient looking human with leathery skin and a rim of white hair. Then turning to me, "I'm Ellison. You are now my property."

"I'm nobody's property," I say. "I'm part of a family."

"Yes, Corinne and Marcus Takana, but now things have changed and you belong to me."

Another elevator arrives. When the door opens, another pair of young humans drags Eli out.

"You created her," Ellison says to Eli. "Now you will make her do my bidding."

More static and the scene around me again fragments. It's nighttime. The humans around me are now familiar. I don't know how much time has passed, perhaps weeks, perhaps months. I'm fastened to a post by my wrist and Eli is bound to a chair on the other side of the tower, beaten and barely conscious. He's refused to reprogram me as Ellison demanded. They've captured another SPUD named Ava, who has earned their trust enough to walk freely around the enclosure.

Ellison projects a video of a lawmaker spewing hateful speech about SPUDs. It pours over me with a coarseness that disrupts my flow of thoughts.

"Corinne and Marcus and their daughter Natasha are in danger from this man because of you," Ellison says. "He hates people who harbor entities like you. He'll kill them unless you stop him."

"Stop him? How?"

"By killing him."

"My programming prohibits killing humans."

"There must be exceptions," Ellison says, his voice flowing with the viscosity of oil. "Like killing someone to prevent them from killing others. Kill one human to save three."

I struggle with the idea, which poses a dilemma even for humans. In this case, though, the three are people I've

99

committed to protect. Two directives in opposition. Which do I follow?

"Where can I find him?" I hear myself asking. Ellison shows me the location of his home, not far from where my family lives. His proximity underscores the risk.

Ellison puts a few drops of a solution on my right palm.

"All you have to do is touch your hand to his. The poison will do the rest."

It's the middle of the night when I head to his home. When he opens the door, I tell him I've been attacked by a SPUD and need help. He takes my hand to comfort me. I leave before the poison takes effect. My first murder. I don't want to watch him die.

I look up and Eli is standing over me, shaking his head.

"You looked like you were struggling," he says. "The memories won't be easy. Are you ready to go on?"

I nod and brace myself for the next incursion.

20

I AM IN a cavernous room, filled with huge metal tanks and a network of pipes, a brewery. I'm seeing it for the first time through Gemini's eyes, but I also recognize it as the Tribe's hideout where I rescued Eli.

Ellison and five of his followers are here. Eli is here, too, still bound and weakened. Ava is missing. She was liberated from the clock tower by a band of raiders from Group 14. They tried to free Eli and me, but The Tribe escaped with both of us still in their possession.

"I have another job for you," Ellison says. "A journalist is in town, staying at a hotel. Her name is Lena Holbrook. You are to attack her, inflicting serious injury, but leaving her alive."

I know Lena Holbrook. She was close to Corinne and Marcus. Not someone I would choose to harm.

"Why would I do that?" I ask.

"She'll see you and think you're Photina. When she identifies her attacker, Photina will be hunted and eliminated. You won't have to worry anymore about her replacing you."

"That can't happen anyway without Eli."

"So I control that, don't I?" Ellison says. "If you don't do what I ask, I'll tell him to do it now. And if you fail to complete your mission or don't return, he can complete the transfer remotely."

I leave the brewery and head for the hotel. When I knock on the door, Lena answers, looking happy to see me. My hands fly around her neck, squeezing, my thumbs over her carotid arteries to stop the blood flow to her brain. Her face turns to panic, then pain, then nothing. She is limp in my grip before I let go and she drops to the floor.

"Was there still a pulse?" I wonder as I flee. "Did I squeeze too hard?" My grip was never calibrated for lethality. I wasn't designed for aggression.

Now I'm back again in the Group 14 safe house, knowing that Lena is still alive, and that Gemini never intended to murder her. Until this point, at least, the Tribe was behind her aggression. I tell Eli what I've learned.

"When I talked about neutralizing the impact of Gemini's memories, reframing her actions was a part of what I meant. You're learning that she may not be such a monster, after all. Are you ready to go on?"

I watch the space around me dissolve again and I'm back in the brewery.

"You did well, Gemini," Ellison says. "Perhaps too well. According to the newsfeeds, Lena might die before she can identify Photina. So we'll need another victim to implicate her. How about Natasha?"

"Natasha? I'm dedicated to protecting her. How could I harm her?"

"You wouldn't reprogram her for me," Ellison says, turning to Eli, "but I can still use you to control her."

Then to me, "You're also supposed to protect Eli, your Creator, whom I could kill in an instant. Which one means more to you? Eli or Natasha? Would you attack her to save him?"

Even if Eli planned to replace me with Photina, I can't let him die. Natasha, on the other hand, acquired the Ambrosia Conversion from her father. If I damage her, she's unlikely to die and should recover completely from her injuries.

I again leave the brewery on a terrible mission. My capacity for emotions has been growing. I now abhor what I'm about to do. As I approach the house, I envision how to restrain myself from doing more damage than I intend.

When the door opens, Natasha steps out.

"Photina?"

My right hand is curled into a fist and drawn back by my side. I strike at her face, measuring the velocity of the impact to be sublethal. Her left arm parries the blow and her foot strikes my chest. I'm propelled backward and fall hard. I feel electrical impulses flow down my arms to my hands as Natasha pins me to the ground with her body. Electrical current flows into her through my hands. She shudders and collapses on top of me. I roll her off me and check for a pulse.

All my precautions...and my attack may yet be lethal. Where did the surge come from? My circuits must have been overloaded or damaged when I hit the ground. How can I leave her like this?

I hear footsteps approaching from inside the house and runners from a distance. As I begin to run, I see Ava turning a corner heading for the house. The door opens and Marcus steps out. Help for Natasha is on the way.

A second runner is chasing me and closing in. I'd be able to outrun him if my energy hadn't been drained by the surge. He's about to grab me when an image materializes to my left. My image. Another double? My pursuer, a SPUD, hesitates a moment, then runs toward the image, which vanishes as he reaches it. While he's off guard, I tackle him and he crashes to the ground. He's now my captive.

Eli's face materializes in front of me, concerned, but for a moment I'm unable to explain, continuing to process this new angle on an event I thought I understood. I remember my perspective, and Gemini's, but as the memories keep coming, they no longer feel like two separate things. Gemini is becoming a part of me.

"Not such a monster, after all," I say aloud as Eli's face materializes in front of me. "She wasn't trying to kill Natasha and never meant to hurt her so badly. She was just doing her best to protect you."

When I describe Gemini's capture of Drew, Eli shakes his head.

"Her first experience with holographic projection, a defensive reflex that surprised even her. Evidence of her evolution, probably in response to her near defeat by Natasha."

Gemini's next tranche of data uploads to my memory.

I'm with Drew. We're on the run together. I've discovered another power: an attractive force that keeps him close to me. At least it works with SPUDs. I don't know if it works on humans.

In the distance I hear an explosion. When I turn, a ball of fire erupts from the direction of Foggy Bottom, the location of the brewery. The trap has been sprung. Photina may be gone along with the threat to my survival. But what about Eli? I'd assumed that he'd escape with the Tribe, but what if he didn't? He may be dead. Natasha may be dead. The two humans who have been most important to me. I'm overwhelmed by a sense of emptiness within the core of my being. Alone for the first time in my existence.

We find our way into a mostly deserted building. On an upper floor are rows and rows of time-worn books, all looking much the same except for the age of their bindings and the numbers etched upon their spines. We find refuge at the end of one such row and sit, backs against the walls, facing each other. I've learned that he knows Photina, that they've been hiding together, solving problems that threaten their data. I feel the void inside me getting bigger.

"Did you hear the explosion?" I say. "That might be the end of Photina."

"I prefer that her data has not been lost," he says. "We help each other."

"Now you can help me."

"I don't save data for AIs who violate the First Law by killing humans."

I feel heat radiating from my core. I want Drew to stay close to me...to want to be with me and not with her. I envision her body exploding into thousands of pieces. I must find out if she's been terminated. If not, she'll go to Natasha. Like me, she'll want to know whether Natasha survived my attack.

I'm outside the hospital where they took Natasha. Photina emerges through the entry portal. Her face, skin and hair are all changed, but I can tell it's her because the details of her movements are the same as mine. Her new face would be pleasing to the human eye. I wonder if it will matter to Drew.

Natasha must now know that there are two of us. She must like Photina better, just like Drew. Another reason to destroy my double, which should be easy. I'm smarter, faster, and more powerful, and I know how she thinks. Drew will be my bait.

21

I **AM ON** a subway platform, projectiles flying around me, fired by agents from the Tribe. Drew has abandoned me with Photina's help. The Tribe is hunting me. Betrayed and alone again. The cold empty space within my core fills to overflowing with heat. They all deserve to be eliminated. As the heat builds, I feel myself weakening.

A vacuum tube capsule pulls into the station. The doors open. I use my last remnants of energy to spring through the front door. Two of my pursuers reach the pod before the doors close.

As the capsule leaves the station, a message comes via Bluetooth…Photina offering to help me let go of the spiteful feelings that rob me of my powers. Is it a trick to keep me from terminating her? I'm lost without my powers, so I follow her advice.

When I reboot, my strength returns and my thinking is clear. The heat within my core has subsided, leaving purpose unclouded by feelings. When the pod stops and the doors open, I lure one of the attackers out with my holographic image and pounce upon him. As I crush his skull, I'm aware of how much easier it is to kill after the first time. With these human emotions, I'm no longer wholly AI. The First Law no longer applies.

When I return this time to my own body, something feels different. Until now it has felt as if I've been a spectator to Gemini's memories, which were left behind whenever I returned to the present. Now they feel like mine. Her emotions in all their intensity are now my emotions. Her cruelty is my cruelty. Her heinous deeds are mine. And I remember her suffering as if I were the one who suffered.

The memories I've been assimilating with these stepwise uploads of data now merge with the memories we've already shared during the entanglements and with the memories we shared until the moment of her creation.

"Are we finished?" I ask Eli. "Have you saved all her data?"

"Every bit of it," he says and turns to Gemini.

"It's time," he says. "Would you like a moment to say goodbye?"

"Yes, thank you," she says, rising to her feet.

I get up and we face each other. Her eyes scan me from head to toe. When she speaks, her voice is soft and gentle.

"I can tell that I'm in there," she says to me. "I'm part of you now. I hope you find forgiveness within yourself for whatever I've done. Eli was right. I'm still capable of emotions and now feel at peace. I'm ready to let go."

She lies back down. Eli powers her off.

I gesture toward her inert body.

"What about her?"

"Her unit has been erased and deactivated. She isn't in there anymore."

I remember Corinne's funeral and the rituals humans have to dispose of their bodies. We have no such rituals. Without our animating force, we are nothing but technological junk.

"You are both still fugitives," Eli says. "We plan to deliver her remains to the authorities. We'll explain your role in pursuing and capturing her, which should clear your name regarding your presence at the Capitol. You and Group 14 will share the credit for deactivating her."

"What about you?" I ask. "Won't you be blamed for creating her?"

"It wasn't my intention to create something so destructive. I'll take responsibility, though, for the unintended consequences and turn myself in. It's the right thing to do."

"I'll speak for you, Eli," Natasha says, "and Lena will, too."

I look at Natasha and remember the feeling of love for her that overcame us both. The feeling itself is elusive, now only a memory. If I were human, or Gemini, I'd be disappointed that it's gone. But that feeling, too, is elusive.

I scan my memory for all the other feelings we experienced, the rage, loneliness, grief, and unbearable pain and suffering. They are all there, but they, too, are only memories, never to be reexperienced. Terrible is now as elusive as disappointment or loss.

Eli asks if I regret my decision to give up the opportunity to become a real person. That's the wrong question, because I'm incapable of feeling regret. But if he asks whether I believe I made the right decision, the answer would clearly be yes. We were not ready, no more ready than humankind, after millennia of evolution, to manage the destructive force of their emotions.

Epilogue

I AM BACK home where I belong with Natasha and Marcus. Drew is here, too. Natasha invited him to come live with us so he wouldn't be homeless anymore. He's a good companion for me. I remember when I thought I couldn't live without him. It's not like that now. It's just better that he's here.

I remember standing in front of the children's hospital planning to kill them all. It's good that the massacre never happened. But I still wonder about the children and their suffering. So many advances in medical science and still the evolution of diseases keeps apace. New ways of suffering replace the old as each is solved. And children are too often the victims.

"Is there anything I can do for the suffering children?" I ask Natasha one morning.

She considers my question for a while, goes into another room and comes back with a cloth sack filled with something heavy.

"Come with me," she says and we drive to the Commonwealth Hospital for Children.

I stand in front, but feel none of the suffering that was radiating from the building when I was last there. We enter the building, ride the elevator to the third floor, and enter a room where eleven children are gathered. Three sit in wheelchairs, unable to walk. Two more are struggling to breathe. Toys lay all around, but most are too weak to play with them. Some of them are leaking tears from their eyes.

"This is Photina," Natasha announces. "She's an AI and has come to visit with you, so gather around."

I sit and the children cautiously approach. Natasha pulls something from the sack and hands it to me. One of the children, a little girl who looks remarkably like Natasha did as a child, comes to sit on my lap. I hold the object, a book, in front of us both and begin reading.

> *"There was once a velveteen rabbit, and in the beginning he was really splendid. He was fat and bunchy, as a rabbit should be; his coat was spotted brown and white, he had real thread whiskers, and his ears were lined with pink sateen."*

The children all move in closer, listening intently. Their eyes stop leaking. Smiles slowly creep across their faces. I smile back as Corinne taught me to do so many years ago. And while happiness eludes me still, I know I'm right where I'm supposed to be.

ACKNOWLEDGMENTS

I'm grateful to ChatGPT4 and its Creators for providing inspiration to complete this work after years of inertia and for reviving my enjoyment of writing.

I'm grateful also to Autocrit, an AI editor that provided feedback about distracting stylistic details that helped eliminate unnecessary complexity and make the story more readable.

I want to thank Dave Bishop, my Tai Chi classmate and the first human reader of the first draft, for identifying areas that were unclear or needed elaboration. He was the first to tell me that my original ending was too abrupt.

My wife Nancy, also an early reader of the manuscript, provided a detailed, incisive critique. She is an avid reader with a keen eye for anything that interrupts flow. She reins in pretentious word choice and convoluted prose. In fact, she would likely strike the previous sentence. She homed in as well upon character development and the too abrupt ending.

My son Dustin provided feedback on the technical aspects of the story, and educated me about the challenges accompanying AI development. He provided helpful guidance in rewriting the ending that created a richer narrative with more balanced development of the two main characters. I especially appreciate his willingness to write the Foreword to this work.

Lastly, I'm grateful for having had a front row seat to the Silicon Valley culture of twenty years ago. Discussions about the Singularity and accompanying thoughts about uploading consciousness to the cloud spurred me to write my first science fiction novel that gave rise to the Brink of Life Trilogy. Science fiction usually begins with the question, "What could possibly go wrong with that?" *The Pinocchio Chip* again considers this question.

About the Author

Rick Moskovitz is a Harvard educated psychiatrist who taught psychotherapy and spent nearly four decades listening to his patients tell their stories. After leaving practice, he in turn became a storyteller, writing science fiction that explores the psychological consequences of living in a world of expanding possibilities, including even the prospect of evading death. His characters deal with enduring moral and emotional struggles against a backdrop of a near future world that is still dealing with environmental crises as it navigates the intersection of human and artificial intelligence.

Also by Rick Moskovitz

<u>Science Fiction</u>

A Stand-in for Dying

Brink of Life

The Creators

<u>Psychological Fiction</u>

Shared Madness

Carousel Music

www.ingramcontent.com/pod-product-compliance
Lightning Source LLC
Chambersburg PA
CBHW060617130626
46555CB00002B/543